Mm

J

Bates, Betty, 1921-
    Ask me tomorrow / Betty Bates. -- 1st
ed. -- New York : Holiday House, c1987.
    135 p. ; 22 cm.
    Summary: Although fifteen-year-old
Paige thinks he is determined to get
away from home and pursue his own
career goals in the big city, thirteen-
year-old Abby confuses the issue by
helping him see his Maine countryside
in a more appreciative way.
    ISBN 0-8234-0659-8

    1. Maine--Fiction. 2. Country life--
Fiction. I. Title

InTV   19 DEC 88   15521565   IVCAbc   87-45329

ASK ME
TOMORROW

ASK ME TOMORROW

Betty Bates

HOLIDAY HOUSE / NEW YORK

020548576

The characters in this book are fictional,
and any resemblance to real persons is
purely coincidental.

Library of Congress Cataloging-in-Publication Data

Bates, Betty
Ask me tomorrow.

Summary: Although fifteen-year-old Paige thinks he is
determined to get away from home and pursue his own
career goals in the big city, thirteen-year-old Abby confuses
the issue by helping him see his Maine countryside in a
more appreciative way.
[1. Maine—Fiction. 2. Country life—Fiction]
I. Title.
PZ7.B29452As   1987   [Fic]   87-45329
ISBN 0-8234-0659-8

For GEORGE and WENDY,
and for everyone on the Hill,
with warm affection and appreciation

ASK ME TOMORROW

ONE

"Morning's going to come early, son. You turn that off and get to bed."

"Oh, come on, Dad, you don't have to remind me." I got up and clicked the TV button, and the screen went blank.

Dad stood in the doorway, almost filling it. He ran a hand over his cheek where the stubble stands out. "Remember, Paige, I'll be wanting you on time when you start work here next week. Got to set the example." His voice is big and raspy, like an engine with no oil.

Every Sunday night, he and I go through the same routine, with me watching *Gibson*, my favorite private-detective show, and him lecturing me about my responsibilities. There was only one more week of school, and then I'd be working for him here on the farm again. This summer would turn out to give me more grief than ever, because it was the summer of Abby Winch. But now it was only June, and my problem was Dad, always bugging me about not getting enough sleep. Okay, so I do get up kind of late some mornings, but I've only been late for school a couple of times. All Dad hears is the sound of his own voice. He won't listen.

My face was burning. It always does when I'm really smoked, or when I'm embarrassed. It freaks me out, and then the red gets redder.

Now, so Dad wouldn't see it, I stamped past him, calling over my shoulder, "You don't have to jump on me the minute *Gibson*'s over. I go up to bed every time."

Well, almost every time. Sometimes, when I went past my sister Joyce's room, I got talking with her about her boyfriend, Earl Sanders, who wanted them to get married when they graduated from high school next June. Lots of their friends were doing it. But Mom and Dad hated the idea. They wanted Joyce to go to college the way they did.

Halfway up the stairs, I looked west out the landing window and past the old section of our farm to the White Mountains across the border in New Hampshire. Closer in were the Maine foothills, with Truitt Hill, our hill, spread out around me. Dad says the Hill will be mine someday, with its crisscross rows of apple trees, the barns, the storage buildings, the packing house, the cider room, the mechanics' shop, the trucks and tractors and three-wheelers, the pickers' barracks, the foreman's place, and the house a little way down the road where Grampa lives. Truitt Hill Orchards, Bartlett, Maine. I suppose I should have felt lucky.

Only he'd never asked me if I wanted them.

Well, I didn't. I didn't want to go rushing around checking on the mowing and grafting and thinning and spraying and irrigating operations, making sure the packing house has bags and the cider room has jugs, worrying about whether the sprays are environmentally okay, and watching to see that the pickers' barracks are ready for the state and union inspections in August. All that busy-work for a bunch of apples.

Dad and Mom never get a chance to go much of anywhere, except to agricultural meetings. They don't seem to really live. And I don't want to be locked in here with boundaries marked on some surveyor's map. I'll go to Portland or, better still, Boston, because it's bigger. I'll be a detective like Gibson, or join the CIA, or be a TV news correspondent or newspaper reporter. I've been getting top grades on my school writing projects. Maybe I could write detective stories.

I want to do something that's me. Something that's for real. I'll be sixteen in December. Instead of being stuck here, where there's never any excitement, I ought to make up my own mind what to do.

I walked up the rest of the stairs. "Psst! Hey, Paige." Joyce was whispering to me from her room. She was wearing that foxy grin of hers that could mean trouble.

"Joyce, I've got to get to bed. Dad'll boil me in oil if he hears me talking."

"Oh, come off it, Paige. You can talk low, can't you?" She was sitting on her four-poster bed combing her just-washed hair. As Gibson would say, she was about five-five. Yellow robe. Short curls the color of applesauce. Roundish face. Blue eyes, average nose, and wide mouth.

The mouth was smiling. Joyce's smile is catching, maybe because she's the kind of person who wakes up in the morning with goose bumps because there's another day waiting for her to shake its hand. She likes who she is, and where she is, and the people she's around. She ought to be a pain, but she's not. She's okay. "I need you to cover for me on Friday night, Paige baby," she said.

Sheez! I'm five-ten already. I'm shaving, and my voice hardly ever cracks, and she's still calling me "Paige baby." Just because she's got two years on me. "Quit calling me that, and maybe I'll listen."

"Okay, this is it. A bunch of us are going down to Portland. There's a car auction Earl's got to go to, and we want to stop at Bean's on the way home. It's no fun if you feel rushed, and we're going to be late getting back, maybe around one in the morning, and you know what pills Dad and Mom are when I get in late."

"Appears to me that's your problem."

"Listen, Paige, all you have to do is put Wiz in the cider room before you go to bed so he won't make a racket." Wiz is our German shepherd who lives outside and barks at everything that moves. "You can tell Dad and Mom, when they get back from the grange supper, that I'm already in bed, and I can sneak in later."

"You know Dad's got watchdog ears."

"He won't hear me, I promise."

"So you want me to stick my neck out for you, right?"

"Earl's going to bid on a car they advertised. If he gets it, you can drive it."

"What's so great about that?"

"It's a BMW, Paige. He says it's got to be a beauty. He's practically frothing at the mouth just from reading about it."

"A BMW, huh? Look, I might not even be here on Friday night. I might be out with my buddies."

"Tell them to come here. Look, you can all go for rides later on."

Now that we had our driver's licenses, I pictured my best friend, Rusty Moreau, and me chauffeuring our friends around in that car, cruising past the houses of other people in our school to impress them.

"So you want me to lie for you and Earl?"

"He's got to have that car, Paige."

Earl is six-three and plays tackle on the Bartlett High football team. He's got a couple of teeth missing, a bump on his nose from having it busted in a game with Alden High, and average report cards. He calls Joyce his eight-cylinder girl, and I think he'd wrestle all the men in this county for her, separately or all at once. Maybe that's one reason she's so crazy about him.

Sure, I like Joyce. But lately she's been kind of sneaky, maybe because of Earl's influence. It's true that my parents watch over her like the FBI. It's stupid. Still, I've got to give them credit for always being honest with us.

Joyce was blinking at me. "Paige, there are times when I'd like to divorce our parents. I mean, they can be so *gross*. So please, Paige. *Please?*"

I pictured that car, all polished and shiny. Black, with a flashy metal bumper and grille, and a hood ornament that socks your eyes out, and it'll go ninety in low gear. Awesome. "Joyce," I finally said, "I'll do it this once. Just this once."

She let out her breath. "Thanks, Paige baby." She stood up and came over and mussed my hair.

"Watch what you call me. I might change my mind."

"You wouldn't. Anyway, you'll be glad you helped us

out. I promise you'll be glad."

Her smile was so warm and sweet she almost had me convinced.

As I walked into my room, stepping over T-shirts and jeans and underwear, I had second thoughts. Why had I told her I'd lie? It's true that Mom and Dad are practically senile, but I didn't want to fib to them. I always turn red and get caught. I flopped on my big old double bed, stuck my feet up on the footboard, stared at the Patriots poster over my bookcase, and realized I'd been conned. There was something about Joyce's everything's-going-to-be-terrific attitude that had hooked me. And now I was stuck.

TWO

I went to the trouble of talking some of my friends into coming over on Friday night to celebrate the end of school. Rusty planned to drive them out from the village, two other boys and three girls.

"Paige," Mom said, "you know I don't want you having that group over here when we're not around."

Sheez! Did she have to be so tough on me?

"Don't you trust us, Mom?"

"No."

I made my sad-clown face, which alway gets her laughing, and she said, "Well, all right. We'll be home early anyway."

Rusty walked in carrying a bag with a couple of six-packs he'd talked his older brother out of. "Okay, you guys," I said, "be careful. Mom and Dad'll be home any minute, and we can't have beer cans sitting around."

We watched *The Blob* on the VCR, with the girls acting scared, and then we sat around the living room eating Mom's date bars and drinking things out of cans. When Stacey English spilled Pepsi on the sofa, we mopped it up and hoped it didn't leave a stain. If Mom

9

saw traces, she'd skin me alive. After Harvey Biggs had pinched Stacey's butt and been given a healthy slap in the face, we knuckled down to business and started talking about the other kids at school.

When we got around to Alvina Fox, who was going into her senior year, Cade Garrison said, "I'll bet half the football team has made out with her."

"Oh, come on, Cade," I said, "you've got no way of knowing." I considered Cade my girl. Had ever since grade school.

She stuck her chin out. "I've heard things."

I wondered if she was as sure of her facts as she pretended to be. "Well," I told her, "I haven't heard much of anything, and I'm on the team. Give Alvina a break. She's okay."

Cade narrowed her eyes at me. "And how come you know so much about her?" Cade was the kind of girl who attracted your attention, with her cornsilk hair curling around her face, and her hazy green eyes, and the right number of freckles marching across her cheeks, and the way she sat with her shoulders straight and her head up. She liked the idea that I was her private property. I liked it too. Whenever she smiled at me, I got goose bumps. Always had. It was as if we had some terrific secret between us.

But she wasn't especially careful when she talked about people outside our crowd. I imagine she could wreck someone's reputation if she felt like it. She may have been right about Alvina, who gets mentioned a lot in the boys' locker room and who had fluttered her eyelids at me a few times last year, even though I was only a freshman. But why pass along rumors?

Cade and I had forgotten about Alvina and were dancing to radio music and giggling at Rusty, who was tossing pieces of date bars at his mouth and mostly missing, when we heard my parents pull up outside. Rusty got down on his knees to pick up his mess while the rest of us got beer cans into the bag fast. We heard Dad go into the barn to take care of some late chore. When Mom breezed in, we were flopped around the room as if we hadn't moved all evening.

Mom talked about how late it was, much later than she'd expected, and she shooed us all out. "Take some date bars with you." My friends didn't need to be encouraged, especially Rusty, who scooped up a handful, stuffed one into his tubby face, grabbed his paper bag, and took off with Mom calling after him, "Tell your mother I'll drop off some applesauce soon as I cook it up on Monday."

"Grmmm," muttered Rusty with his mouth full. The screen door slammed behind him.

I went out to say goodbye. Wiz got up from lying next to the mailbox and tagged after me. Everyone piled into Rusty's Toyota except Cade, who held back. "'Bye, Paige." She brushed against me, almost as if it were an accident.

I couldn't resist giving her a quick kiss. "'Bye, beautiful."

Her smile went all through me. "See you tomorrow at the pond?"

"Sure. Same time, huh?"

"Right." The smile was lasting a long time.

"Hey, you lovebirds, let's slip it into gear." It was Rusty, waiting to leave, drumming his fingers on the steering wheel.

Cade turned and walked to the car, head up, taking her time.

As they pulled away, I took hold of Wiz's collar and led him into the cider room. While I was closing the door on him, he tipped his head and gave me a forlorn look. I felt mean. Going back across the yard, I could hear his whining.

Inside, Mom was bringing Pepsi cans out of the living room. "I don't suppose Joyce got home," she said.

I felt the blush come into my face, so I waited till she passed me before I answered. "She came home and went to bed," I said. "She must have been tired."

"Can't believe that boy actually brought her back at a decent hour." She'd pass my lie on to Dad when he came in, thank goodness. If I'd told it again, they'd have guessed for sure.

The next morning I let Wiz out of the cider room before breakfast. He jumped all over me, so maybe he wasn't too mad. Joyce and I ate at the beat-up walnut table that goes back in our family practically to the time of the *Mayflower*. Mom was in the kitchen frying sausages, and Dad was out in the packing house checking bags and boxes for Monday's work.

"Did Earl get the car?" I asked Joyce, keeping my voice down.

She sighed and shook her head. "But thanks, Paige. Thanks for covering for me." She gave me that melting smile of hers.

So the whole thing was a washout. My lie hadn't been any use. Besides, it's not every day you get to ride in a BMW. I should have known, though. Earl's always getting big ideas about cars that don't work out. "Have any trouble sneaking in?" I asked.

"Uh-uh. Easy as pie."

Our parents sleep on the first floor, and if she came in the side door and through the combination dining room and family room, which everyone usually does, she'd have had to go past their room to get to the stairs. They must have been knocked out.

"Too bad about the car."

"Yeah. Earl was outbid right at the start. He couldn't begin to compete, poor guy."

I didn't feel sorry for him. He's got a perfectly good second-hand Camarro with only one problem. It burns oil as if it's going to explode any minute. But what can you expect?

"Guess what, Paige. Earl wants to give me a ring. An engagement ring."

"Yeah?" If Joyce marries Earl, maybe he'd like to take over the farm and get me off the hook, even though Dad turned him down for a summer job. "That Earl Sanders wouldn't know a tree from a truck," Dad had said. So this summer Earl was working at the Exxon station on Route 17.

"You going to take the ring?" I asked Joyce.

"I don't know. Whenever I'm with him, I'm positive I want to marry him. But when I'm not, I just don't know." Her eyes misted up. "He's really smart, Paige. It's just that he's slow when he talks and moves, so people like Dad don't understand how quick he is inside.

And he's as gentle as can be. He wouldn't hurt a flea."

Dad was wiping his feet at the side steps. He came in through the screen door, tossed his cap onto the rolltop desk next to a pile of bills, glanced at the pieces of the white shorts Joyce was making that were on the sewing machine, and came over to sit at the table. Under the line of tan that cut across the middle of his forehead, there were frown lines. He took off his glasses and stared at us. "Heard a car come up the hill around one this morning. Stopped down around Winches' place. Either of you know whose it was?" His voice was raspier than ever, the way it gets when he's angry.

The car had probably been Earl's. He must have let Joyce off partway down the hill near the foreman's place, thinking the sound of his engine wouldn't wake Mom and Dad.

I stared at my plate, with biscuit crumbs stuck in what was left of my egg yolks. Joyce didn't say a word. When I looked up, she was swallowing. I thought she was going to burst into tears. This wasn't like her. I guess she'd thought she and Earl had fooled Dad a sight better than they had.

Mom called from the kitchen. "Might have been the Winches' granddaughter coming in, Ned. She's due one of these days."

Dad shook his head. "Not before the end of the week, I'm told. Couldn't have been her." He grabbed the edge of the table and leaned forward. He seemed to look straight through Joyce. His voice was tight, pounding out the words. "Heard somebody come in the front door and take off up the stairs. By the time I got to the hall, the person was out of sight. Any idea who it might have been?"

So she'd snitched a key to the front door so she wouldn't have to sneak past the downstairs bedroom. But Dad doesn't miss anything. I'll bet he can hear an apple drop all the way over in Ingram Field.

After what seemed like a month, a voice said, "It was me, Dad." The voice was Joyce's. A tear was wandering down her cheek.

"You're grounded through next weekend, Joyce." He shoved the words at her.

Mom came in with sausages for her and Dad. She sat down, shaking her head at Joyce. "I wondered how come Wiz wasn't around when I got up this morning. Where was he, Paige?"

Everyone looked at me. My mouth went dry. "Just over in the cider room."

"He's never slept in the cider room," said Mom. "Joyce got you in on this, didn't she? You told me she was already in last night."

"You let Joyce make you into a liar?" Now Dad only looked sad and tired. He turned to Mom. "What do you think, Lou?"

"Well, he's too old for a paddling, but I expect you'll bawl him out good and proper."

Dad shook his head. "I thought we could trust you, Paige."

"You can, Dad. It was only this once."

"Well, I don't know what to say to you. It's certain you know how disappointed we are." He was wearing his how-can-you-do-this-to-me look. "Paige, if you can't be honest and straightforward, how do you expect to run this farm someday?"

Now, what was I supposed to say to that?

THREE

The Garrisons have a camp at Piney Pond, where my crowd spends Saturday afternoons and evenings in the summers. It's a two-room cabin with a porch, a beach, a motorboat, and a wind-surfer. There were nine of us there that afternoon in bathing suits, including Cade's eight-year-old brother, a small hunk of dynamite named Dennis. Cade's parents had left her in charge while they went down to Portland for shopping and supper.

Cade's a natural at wind-surfing. She never tips over. In a white tank suit that showed off her curves, she swooped from side to side, with her blond hair shining like the flame of some candle. While the rest of us watched from shore, Rusty gave a low whistle. "Get a load of those, um, legs," he said, darting a look at Stacey English.

I'd brought my Nikon along and was snapping pictures. As Cade made a smooth landing, I got one of her. "Nice going," I told her.

Dennis jumped up and down. "My turn. My turn."

"No, Dennis," said Cade as I helped her beach her board, "it's Paige's turn."

"That's okay," I said. "Dennis can go."

"But he doesn't know how."

"You mean he's never done wind-surfing?"

"Of course not."

"Then I'll teach him."

"Paige, he's much too young."

"You're never too young to learn, huh, Dennis?"

"Right." He was smiling.

Cade shrugged. "If anything happens to him, you can blame yourself." She walked away quickly.

I set my camera down, and with Dennis on the board, I shoved it out in the water, turning it so the sail would catch the wind, and steadying it. I stood Dennis in front of me and laid my hands over his. We stayed close to shore, moving back and forth, and after a few minutes Dennis began to get the feel of the surfer. I was barely touching his arms. Cade came to the edge of the sand, her hands on her hips, her head back. She always seemed sure of herself, in control, expecting people to go along with her. And they nearly always did. "Okay, Paige, let's get it over with. Come on in."

She could be just plain bossy.

"He's catching on, Cade. He's doing fine."

"That's enough, though. Mom'll have a fit as it is."

Mrs. Garrison's an awful worrier. And after all, Cade's parents had left her in charge. Naturally she didn't want any accidents. Besides, it was her surfer. I brought Dennis in, and the rest of us took our turns. I did all right, surfing to the middle of the pond where the breeze was strongest, and around in figure eights, feeling the wind on my chest and the tapping of the ripples under my feet.

When Rusty took his turn, he acted kooky and tried to navigate on one foot. The board tipped over, and I ran the boat out to rescue him. He puffed as he climbed in. "Hey, Truitt, how come I can't get that thing to stay up?"

"Too much of your mom's chocolate cake, Moreau. Try living clean, like the rest of us."

Then Cade went out to do her number again, and when she came in she said it was time to eat the hot dogs and potato chips Harvey Biggs had brought because it was his turn. The rest of us had chipped in munchies and fruits and cookies from home. We built a fire in the grill, and as we roasted our hot dogs, there was a lot of kidding and shoving around. When Harvey and Rusty tried sneaking out of the cabin with a six-pack of Mr. Garrison's beer, Cade called out, "You two want to get asked back?"

Her dad would be sure to miss that beer. "Stay out of that cabin," I said, "unless you need to pee."

Everyone laughed, and the boys took the beer back.

After supper, Harvey and I threw Rusty off the pier. There was more horseplay till Cade's folks drove up around nine. As Mr. Garrison got out of the car, Dennis ran up to him. "I wind-surfed! I wind-surfed! Paige taught me how."

His dad, who was carrying a big paper bag from Porteus department store, gave him a bear hug. "Good for you, Dennis."

Mrs. Garrison screwed up her round face as if she'd eaten a pickle. "I declare that boy's going to an early grave." Her husband followed as she carried her packages inside, shaking her head.

Cade and I always did a lot of kissing when we got the chance, but we didn't get a chance that night. She and I moved away from the group, but Dennis stuck to me like hair oil. I hadn't counted on making such a close friend of him, at least not now. "Go inside, Dennis," Cade kept saying. "It's your bedtime."

"It is not my bedtime."

"See?" said Cade. "He's a pest." She gazed off toward the far side of the pond, where the pine trees were hazy silhouettes. "Everything's so stupid here. I want to get out the minute I graduate from high school." She leaned against me. She felt soft and comfortable. "Don't you, Paige, hm?"

"You bet I do."

I could feel the magic between us. Neither of us had actually said it, but I think we both had a fuzzy notion we'd get married someday. Still, I didn't want it to be right after high school. I planned to go to college. Would she wait till I finished?

Joyce was going to be working in the packing house again that summer, and Dad had put me with one of the crews that move from field to field doing thinning, pruning, and other chores. When I joined my group, they were thinning the Lodi apples over in Ingram Field, which Dad had bought a couple of years ago. It was on another hill, across the valley from ours, and each morning they rode over in cars. The men were wiry and tough, and suntanned already, more than Harvey Biggs and me, who'd been in school. He could run like lightning, and he was already a first-string halfback on our high school football team. Tall and weedy and all sharp angles, with his arms sticking out of his shirtsleeves and his jeans too short.

Near the end of the day, my muscles ached. I was tired of snipping the stems of those dumb, hard little apples. I scooped a handful off the ground and tossed them at Harvey's back.

"Ouch!" He turned to see what had attacked him, but I was busy snipping. After I'd done the same thing to him a couple more times, he caught on. "All right, you old weasel you." He fired a couple of apples at my chest. They stung. I fired back. Gradually the others joined in, and soon there was open warfare, with Harvey laughing so hard it seemed as if he could be heard back at the Big House. I was groping for apples to throw when I saw Dad drive up in the Subaru. He got out and walked toward us and waited as, one by one, the men saw him and went quiet. "You men are working an extra half hour today," he said quietly. "You think that's fair?"

We worked an extra half hour.

At supper that evening, Dad said, "Paige, you know I don't mind your having a good time, but I won't tolerate it when it cuts into the hours I'm paying you for. You'll be turning sixteen in six months, and I expect you to set the example. You got that?"

"Dad, it gets monotonous out there, working in that hot sun."

"I never said it was easy." He dropped the subject and turned to Mom. "Got to go down to Boston Friday to see Coates at the produce center. Might as well take him that last load of Delicious out of the storage." He gave me a sideways look. "Want to come, Paige? You and I could get a lobster for dinner, maybe do some sightseeing, and go see the Red Sox that evening."

Sure, I wanted to go. Couldn't wait.

FOUR

On Friday morning I woke up to the promise of sunshine and the muffled talk of the truck drivers out in the yard that's formed by the L of the Big House and the barn. Every weekday they come in the darkness to pick up apples and cider to deliver to the grocery stores in our part of Maine and over in New Hampshire. Usually I sleep soundly in my creaky old bed, but today I was on edge. The zooming of their engines as they took off, and their clatter going downhill, kept me awake.

After breakfast, a little before seven, when I went out to the truck Dad and I were taking, farm hands and packers were pulling in for work. Wiz greeted each of them with a yelp and a tail wag. I climbed into the seat of the truck, with TRUITT HILL ORCHARDS printed on its side. Sam Winch, the foreman, walked up the road from his house. He'd worked for us for years. Around sixty, I figure. Solid and weather-beaten, with muscles like tree limbs. Dad stopped to make sure Sam had his instructions straight. "Spraying at Puckett and mowing at Henright." Dad called each field by the

name of the family who'd owned it before we Truitts
had bought it. Lots of farmers' children had taken off
for the city over the past years, and their parents had
sold the farms when they retired.

Sam nodded. "Yup." He never said much, but his
blue eyes were sharp under his thick eyebrows.

Dad climbed into the truck next to me. Sitting up so
high, I could see all around. I could see Mom's garden
on the south slope by our house, from the hollyhocks
down to the cabbage plants. I could see Grampa working in the kitchen of his place, washing up from breakfast. And farther along, on the west side of the road, I
could see the Winches' dog, Noodles, snoozing on their
front steps. Behind and around the Winches' house is
Henright Field, where the original orchards are.

Mom came running out waving a couple of windbreakers, Dad's and mine. "You hold on, Ned Truitt.
You take these along. Could be fixing to rain before
you get back tonight."

"No sign of rain, Lou."

"Well, it's bound to get chilly anyway. I don't want
you two shivering yourselves to bits." She handed the
windbreakers up to me, standing on tiptoe. "Now, you
take care, you hear?"

Her cheekbones looked extra-high from where I sat,
and the top of her brown hair was mussed from the
breeze that whips the top of our hill.

As the truck rumbled past Grampa's house and the
Winches' place, with Noodles barking and running
alongside us, the fresh smell of grasses and clover hit
us. Around the bend in the road where the woods
begin, Dad looked off to the right past a clump of ferns

into the pines and birches, oaks and cedars. "Got to get
the underbrush out of there."

"Why, Dad? Why do you keep the woods? They're no
good to anybody."

"They're not, huh? They keep us in firewood. And
they came in some handy during the thirties Depres-
sion when my grandfolks sold off cedars to keep the
family in baked beans and pie dough."

Dad knows every rock and tree on our land, the way
Grampa does, and their forefathers did. All the way
back to the Ark, I suppose. Dad likes to talk about the
old days. If you let him get started, he'll go back to the
time John and Rebecca Truitt came up from Massachusetts and built the house where the Winches live
now. He'll tell about how the Truitt descendants bought
up more land and planted more orchards. How they
built the Big House at the top of the hill, our house,
and attached the barn to it. How his great-grandfather
worked the place with a pair of horses and his great-
grandmother cooked the workers' noon dinner and
room-and-boarded the pickers when they came. How
Great-Aunt Cornelia, who had the gift of the dowsing
rod, had located the family well. How, when he was a
boy, he'd been chased up a tree by an angry cow.

He always puts a lot of loving warmth into that talk,
but sometimes I get bored with it.

Now he took off his cap, set it on the seat between us,
and asked, "How's the work going, Paige?"

Thank goodness he wasn't going to give me another
history lesson.

We bumped along, talking about the men I worked
with. Whose wife was having a baby, who was building a

house over on the Huntville road, and who had just buried a relative. Dad drove through Milton, turned onto the thruway, and concentrated on the road. He wasn't one for a whole lot of small talk.

We hit the Boston area about ten. There's something about that place that makes my spine tingle. All those streets going every which way. Cars and buses and shops and restaurants. Horns honking, brakes screeching, people hollering. All kinds of noises, to exercise my ears for a change. And I could see cops, loafers, fat women in sun dresses, skinny men in tight jeans, kids eating ice-cream cones.

We drove straight to the produce center in Chelsea, which was a madhouse. There were trucks everywhere, with state licenses from different parts of New England. I even saw a Michigan plate. Inside the gate, we waited in line till we could back up to the Bell & Coates section of the long loading platform. As we got out of the truck and hustled up the ladder, a man came forward from the doorway. He was around five-seven. Heavy mustache. Thick arms. "Morning, Sid," said Dad.

Sid nodded. "Made it in good time, I see. The men'll unload."

"Appreciate that. You remember my son Paige."

"He's grown."

"Yup. We'll go see Coates, son. You might as well learn a thing or two."

There it was again, the learning thing, the expecting me to carry on, to keep track of all the unimportant details. It was like having pebbles in my boots. Something extra to worry about. "Dad, I don't care about learning the business."

He gave me a sharp look. "Well, you ought to. It's time, Paige." He walked inside.

I ought to stop him. I ought to shout, make him listen to me, force him to understand. But this wasn't the right time. There was never a right time.

I sighed and followed him through the wide doorway and across a concrete floor with crates here and there. Off to our right was the refrigerated storeroom, from which our apples would be picked up, probably by noon, and delivered to stores. Dad mostly brokers his own apples, sending them around in our trucks, but sometimes he sells extras to Mr. Coates.

Now we clattered up an iron staircase to an office that overlooked the warehouse. Mr. Coates, in his shirtsleeves, got up to meet us. He was around fifty. Six-two. A hundred eighty-five pounds of muscle. Bald. Gray eyes that blinked, big nose, warm smile, strong handshake. Nearly broke my bones.

Now he shook hands with Dad. "Good to see you, Ned."

"You remember Paige," said Dad.

"He's grown," said Mr. Coates, smiling.

I suppose Mr. Coates also expected me to be running the farm someday. He was probably estimating how much muscle I had under my shirt and how many brains I had in my head.

We scraped three chairs into place. Dad had agreed to take over the Perry orchard on the other side of Bristol for spraying and picking, on commission, be-

cause Mr. Perry was ailing. He was also one of the
farmers in our neighborhood who'd been running into
financial problems, and it hadn't helped that he was
laid up. Could Mr. Coates broker the Perry apples?
Dad wondered. Mr. Coates thought he could. As he
and Dad wrote down a lot of figures, Dad kept taking
off his glasses and putting them back on. Finally Mr.
Coates nodded. He'd check out his connections and
give Dad a call. Could we stay and have dinner with
him at the cafeteria down the way?

"Appreciate the invitation," said Dad, "but no
thanks. I promised Paige we'd have a proper lobster
dinner."

We went to a place called The Top Drawer, which
was another madhouse, with wooden tables and booths
and waiters charging around carrying trays. One of the
men at the table next to us had a checked cap, the kind
Gibson wears. A detective, maybe. Dad and I ordered
whole boiled lobster, baked potatoes, and tossed salad.
While I was eating, I thought of the lobstermen I'd
seen sometimes at places along the coast. Maybe I'd be
a fisherman.... Nah. I'd heard that sometimes they go
out on their boats for months. I wouldn't go for that.
It'd probably be too quiet, the way the orchards are too
quiet.

"Name your dessert, Paige." Dad was sitting back
and grinning at me. "Something with ice cream and
nuts, I'll wager."

I discovered I'd eaten every bite of food on my plate
but the shells, even the meat from the lobster legs. I
also discovered I still had an empty space in my stomach. "Right. Hot fudge with the works." I never get hot

fudge at home. Mostly I just get different kinds of pie.

Dad took me to see Bunker Hill and the U.S.S. *Constitution*. Seems one of our ancestors fought at Bunker Hill, so of course Dad had to go and embarrass me by jawing with the guide about our family history, and I had to pretend I wasn't with him. But the *Constitution* was interesting, with the crew's quarters and the cannons and all.

We drove over to Fenway Park in plenty of time to eat hot dogs before the game. A sharp breeze had come up, and I had to admit to myself I was glad to have the windbreaker after all. The Sox lost to the Orioles, six to four, but Wade Boggs got two RBI's and a run, and I got pretty excited. Maybe I'll be a sportswriter.

On the way home, Dad said, "I ought to bring you down here with me more often. Time you learned the marketing end of the business."

I didn't want to spoil his day, so I didn't say anything. I just felt sick inside.

It was after one in the morning when we drove up Truitt Hill. Noodles barked when we got close to the Winches', and a light went on in the south bedroom. A face showed up at the window, the face of a girl who looked ten or eleven.

"Must be the Winches' granddaughter in from Texas," said Dad.

"Hey, that's right. What's her name?"

"Couldn't say. But I expect your curiosity will get you the answer before long."

I expected it would.

FIVE

I didn't need to ask questions, because the next morning at breakfast, Mom said, "Abby Winch is here. Came in yesterday."

"So I see," said Dad.

Sam Winch's wife works at the packing house. I supposed she'd taken the day off yesterday to go to Portland to meet her granddaughter. The Winches' married son lives someplace in Texas, so the girl had come a long way.

Since it was Saturday morning, I took one of the Honda three-wheelers out of the machine shed to ride over to Rusty's in the village, dropping my football in the basket to toss around. I gunned the motor and chugged along cross-country, through Puckett Field and down the woods path where the trucks dump cider mash, and past Butterworth Field to where Laurabell lives, this side of the creek. She was out in her vegetable garden, hunched over, thinning onions. She had on her beat-up straw hat over a coffee-colored face that was crumpled like a popped balloon. Dress a million years old, with flowers all over it. Bare stick legs. Dirty sneakers. Laurabell and her husband, Billy, had come up from Mississippi looking for jobs back in the thirties, and they'd never gone back. They'd worked in the packing house, where Billy had ended up as foreman, and together they'd cleared a piece of land on our place, put up a gray clapboard cabin, planted a garden. I don't remember Billy. He died when I was small.

On either side of Laurabell's steps was a bed of marigolds bordered in smooth rocks. Her copper-and-white cat, Calico, who'd been sunning herself on one of the rocks, came and rubbed against my legs. I leaned down to pet her.

Laurabell looked up at me, shielding her eyes from the sun. "Morning, paleface," she said with a chuckle.

I grinned at her. "Your marigolds look okay, Laurabell, but do you actually expect vegetables to grow in that weed patch of yours?"

"Now, you listen to me, Paige Truitt. I been growing squash bigger than your head for better than forty years."

This was the way she and I always talked, in a kidding way, pretending we had no respect for each other. Now she stood up slowly, very slowly, breathing hard.

"You okay, Laurabell?"

"Nothing ever the matter with me."

"I can go past Biggs's Grocery. Need anything? Like canned green beans?"

"Canned green beans." She spat at the ground, as I had expected she would. "You know I got enough garden beans put up to last me till the Day of Judgment." She smiled, showing me her few teeth, like the dots on dominoes. "Thank you kindly, Mister Truitt, but I

biked to the village yesterday for our necessaries. Callie
and me is doing fine." Calico was called Callie for short.
Laurabell liked to speak of her as if she were a member
of her family, maybe the daughter she'd never had.
Laurabell glanced at the football. "So get along with
you, and take your pleasure." She had a voice like
music. Like an old song.

"I'll do that, Laurabell. You two look after yourselves." I glanced at the neat rows of seedlings, at the
battered watering can, at the ancient bike propped
against the side of the cabin, at the slatted wooden
chair she kept under her kitchen window so she and
Callie could sit and watch the sunsets.

I rumbled away, thinking of all the times Laurabell
had planted that garden, how many suns she'd watched
go down behind the woods, and how many snowy
winters she'd fed wood into that old iron stove of hers.
She'd become a part of the place, like the trees and the
chipmunks and the ghosts of my ancestors.

At the Moreau house, Rusty's big brother, washing
his dad's appliance service truck, told me Rusty was out
in back.

Rusty and I tossed the football around, and after I'd
worn him out, we sat on the grass drinking ginger ale. I
always tease him about his weight, but it never appears
to bother him. He just smiles and changes the subject
and talks. He's the all-time talking champ. Now he went
on and on. About the used Toyota he'd picked up a
month ago. About his dad's appliance service. But
mostly about girls. I put in a "Hm," or "No kidding" at
the proper places. With Rusty and girls it was mostly
chatter and no action.

When it was time for me to go home for noon dinner, Mrs. Moreau tucked a jar of her strawberry preserves in with my football. "Greet your parents for me," she said, smiling so her cheeks were puffier than ever.

As I rode back along our woods path, I saw the girl sitting on a log at the ledge that looks out over Butterworth Field and the creek to the village, with the church spire sticking up over the houses. I guess she'd been watching me come.

She was wearing a striped shirt and jeans, and she was curled in on herself, hugging her knees against her flat chest with her skinny arms. She looked like an elf. Long, dark hair. Bangs. Sharp chin. Peanut nose. Big puddle eyes.

I stopped the three-wheeler and straddled it. "Hi," I said.

She lifted her chin. "Hello." Her voice was fuzzy and soft, like an old quilt.

"What are you doing out here?"

She smiled. "Watching things. I was watching you. You're Paige, aren't you?"

"Right. What's your name?"

"Abby."

"How old are you?"

"That's a rude question, but I'll tell you anyway. I'm thirteen."

Thirteen! She was a lot older than I'd thought. And who did she think she was, telling me I was rude? I was less than impressed.

Her eyes seemed to go on forever. They gave her a spooky look that made me wonder if she came from another planet. But only for a second. I came back to reality. "So would you think it's rude if I ask you where you came from?"

"Texas."

"I already know that. Where in Texas?"

"San Antonio. My dad's in flour. He's rich." She turned and looked out over the speckled tops of the apple trees in Butterworth Field. "You're lucky to live here. My grandfather says you'll be running these orchards someday."

"Maybe I will and maybe I won't."

Her eyes went wide. "You mean you don't want to?"

"Not especially. Only I don't know what would happen to the place if I didn't."

She set her pointy chin on her fist and thought for a minute. "It's like being a prince, isn't it?"

"A prince? You're putting me on."

"I mean it's like being the heir to a throne, and you're expected to take the kingship some day or your family and your subjects will be disappointed in you."

It was true that we Truitts were looked up to around Bartlett. Half the people in the village worked for us, so of course everyone at school knew who I was, and that was tough on me. But in the past few years, more and more outsiders had built houses in our area and were commuting twelve miles south to Milton. Still, even though she sounded kooky, she was right as far as the farm was concerned. If I didn't carry it on, a lot of livelihoods and hopes would collapse. "Well, yeah. Yeah, that's sort of how it is." I threw a leg over the motorbike and sat on the seat sideways.

"What's that over there?" she asked, pointing.

"Cider mash."

"What's cider mash?"

She certainly was loaded with questions.

"Cider mash is what's left after they make cider. They dump it here."

"Do the animals in the woods like it?"

"Sure. Sometimes they even get drunk on it."

She giggled. "Drunk as a skunk, huh?"

"Mm."

She inspected me carefully, narrowing her eyes. "Have you ever seen a bear up close, Paige?"

"Yup. A big one." My voice cracked on the word *big*, but she didn't seem to notice.

"Where were you?"

"Close to here. In the woods."

"Were you frightened?"

"Nah. He went his way, and I went mine." I didn't mention that the bear had been loping along the other side of the ledge, downwind. Of course I wasn't scared. Only a touch nervous.

"There aren't any bears in San Antonio. There's no cider mash either, and there aren't any mountains."

"Yeah? Well, there must be lots of terrific things, though. Like the Alamo. And skyscrapers and fancy restaurants. Also dope pushers and other criminals."

"Criminals? Haven't you got those around here?"

"Well, there was the time Mrs. Garrison caught some man slipping out of the gate with a basket full of tomatoes from her garden. Turned out he was passing through from Milton and liked the look of her vegetables."

Abby giggled. "Paige," she said, turning those big eyes on me, "would you climb a mountain with me?"

What kind of trap was this?

"Maybe, sometime. Hey, I've got to get back for dinner. Want a ride?"

She looked puzzled. "Dinner?" Then her face cleared. "Oh, that's right. Everyone around here eats dinner at noon." She got onto the three-wheeler behind me and wound her thin arms around my waist. She smelled of Ivory soap. When I dropped her off at the Winch place, I said, "Say, um, Abby, I'd appreciate it if you didn't mention to anybody that I might not take over the orchards."

"You mean you haven't told your parents?"

"Nope. Don't want to hurt their feelings unless I'm forced into it."

"I won't tell, Paige. Thanks for the ride. It was splendid."

Splendid? What kind of person had I got mixed up with? I'd told her things I'd never mentioned to anyone, not even to Cade or Rusty. It was as if she were weaving some kind of mystic spell. Except she comes from plain old San Antonio, Texas.

Earl came over the next evening to see Joyce, who'd been grounded through the weekend. From the living room, where I was watching *Gibson,* I heard her letting him in the side door with her usual breathless "Oh, Earl, I'm so glad to see you!"

His galumphing steps passed through our dining-sitting room. "Evening, Mr. Truitt, Mizz Truitt." The footsteps clomped down the hall, and I saw him turn right into the west parlor, followed by Joyce. I thought he was going to knock over my great-grandma's sewing stand. When he's in our house, he reminds me of the Garrisons' Guernsey bull.

He stayed till after Dad and Mom and I had gone to bed. Finally, around eleven or so, I got waked up by Dad calling out, "Earl Sanders, you going to work in the morning?"

"Sure, Mr. Truitt. Why?"

"You planning to go home?"

"Oh, um, sure, Mr. Truitt. Guess I'd better be going."

Whenever Earl's around Joyce, or around a truck or car, he loses track of time.

I fell asleep wishing life were as simple for me as it seems to be for Joyce. She doesn't dream about leaving Bartlett and moving out into the world. She'll probably marry Earl and have six kids and cook and sew and do their laundry and be happy.

In a way I envy her.

I woke the next morning to the sound of rain hitting our roof and washing down the hill. By the time I got to breakfast, Mom and Dad and Joyce were at the table. "We're working inside today, huh, Dad?" I asked.

"Yup. Machine shed needs repairs, and the apples need rain. We're fortunate."

"Last night," said Joyce, "I told Earl I might marry him. He's—" She gave a dreamy sigh. "Well, I just think we're right for each other, that's all."

So it was nearer to being settled. Dad and Mom exchanged looks. They'd probably expected she'd go on to college, that she'd marry a college man. I'll bet she could have almost anyone she wanted. Why was she setting her heart on Earl?

"Joyce," said Dad, "have you thought this over?"

"Uh-huh. I've thought and thought, and I can't think myself out of it. I want to."

Mom set her fork down and asked in a shaky voice, "You didn't get engaged, did you?"

"No. I still might go up to State. But even if I do, I'll end up marrying Earl. There could never be anybody else." She sprinkled salt on her eggs. "I don't really want college, though, Mom. You know I'm no student. Anyway, I've got months to make up my mind about that. He wants to get married after graduation."

"Good," said Dad. "That'll give you almost a year to think some more." He got up, leaving his eggs half eaten, and clomped outside in his heavy boots. He stood like a big bear in the drizzle, rubbing his chin, looking west toward the mist covering the mountains.

Would he be that upset if I told him about my plans for the future? I could probably count on it.

SIX

By Saturday morning it was warm and clear. Blue sky. Hot sunshine. I could make out the top of Mount Washington, way over in New Hampshire. Mom sent me over to Grampa's to pile up the firewood one of the men had dumped next to his side porch. "Now, you be careful of your back, you hear?" said Mom. "Don't lean over. Flex your knees."

I rolled my eyes toward heaven. "Sure, Mom." She should have made a tape of those three sentences.

My grampa's sort of slowed down with arthritis and a bad heart. Mom worries that he'll do too much, and the more jobs we take over, the smaller his muscles get.

It must be hard on him, not being able to do much physical labor. He used to get out and work with the men. It had been his idea to build the first of our four storage buildings, and he helped put it together. Now he runs errands for the farm and handles the books. He and Dad are partners.

As I crossed the yard, a swallow flew out of the barn and swooped over a pile of boards that sat ready for a shelf repair job in the packing house. There were tire tracks leading to the gas pump and a tractor outside the mechanics' shop waiting for an engine job.

I went past Grampa's pickup truck, through his side porch, and in at the door off his kitchen, where he was rinsing his breakfast dishes. He's not all that big. Around five-nine. Thin gray hair. Bark-brown eyes. Hooked nose. Creased cheeks. Gnarled hands. Green-and-brown plaid shirt. Pants worn thin at the knees. Boots scuffed all over. "You didn't need to come, Paige. Not that I'm not some glad to see you."

"That's all right, Grampa. You get the payroll out okay?"

"Never missed yet. Hope I never will."

There was a knock at the front door. Grampa looked puzzled. Nobody ever knocks at his front door. "I'll get it," I said.

When I opened up, there stood Abby. She had on a baby-blue shirt hanging loose over her jeans and a straw hat tied under her chin that was about a mile wide. She looked as if she'd break when you touched her. She grinned. "I saw you coming over here."

What was she doing chasing me around? Well, I'd show her. "You're just in time. You can help pile firewood on the porch."

"Good." She practically leaped in the door, knocking her hat to one side on the frame. Her nose twitched. "Blast!" She straightened the hat. "I have to wear this on account of the sun. I burn easily. I have very sensitive skin."

Somehow I didn't feel like crying.

Grampa had come to see what the excitement was. "Hello," said Abby. "I'm Abby."

"Well, Abby, you look like a regular farmer, an extra-pretty one."

Pretty? Scrawny was more like it.

A pink blush showed on her very sensitive skin. "I'm going to help Paige with the firewood," she said.

Grampa dug his fists into the pockets of his pants and looked her over some more. He hated needing to be helped. It must have hurt to have a city girl like Abby offering to do his work. But it does get chilly some summer evenings on the Hill, and chances were good he'd need a fire now and then. Besides, the wood was a mess out back.

He nodded and said quietly, "All right, Abby." He turned and walked through the kitchen and into his office, and we heard the *click-click* of his calculator as he figured the Truitt Hill Orchards accounts.

For such a puny person, Abby didn't do badly lifting bunches of cut branches.

"You're awfully messy, Paige." She took the sticks I'd just dumped and arranged them neatly side by side at the top of our pile. When we were nearly done, she carried the rest of the wood into the house and set it in the box by the living-room fireplace. That was something I had never thought to do.

After we'd washed our hands at the kitchen sink, she turned to me. "What'll we do now?"

We? What did she mean, we? I had some unfinished business before I went to Piney Pond that afternoon.

"I'm planning to go home and finish reading my *Sports Illustrated*," I said.

"*Sports Illustrated*?" She pronounced the words as if they were poison.

"Yeah. Say, have you got a hearing problem?"

She shuddered. "Paige, you're not going to stay inside on such a hauntingly beautiful day. You ought to be outside feeling the warm sun and fresh air."

Sheez! I get enough sun and air during the week.

I shifted into reverse. "Look, Abby, if you don't like baseball articles, it's all the same to me. Nobody's stopping you from going ahead and feeling the sun and fresh air."

The clicking of Grampa's calculator had stopped. "You think Abby might like to be shown Bible Corner, Paige?"

Bible Corner is at the junction of two ancient stone walls in the woods off Tinker Field. Way back when my great-great-grandfather was running our place, he had a fuss with his neighbor about a boundary. When they settled the argument and built walls, they put a Bible between some stones in the corner where the walls joined. The Truitts ended up buying the neighbor's property, but the Bible stayed. I guess it's supposed to be a sort of symbol, a reminder that we need to get along with our neighbors.

That first Bible almost fell apart and had to be replaced years ago, but Grampa sticks in a new one every so often with a yellow page pressed inside that came from the original. He's fierce about it, and reverent. Partly out of respect for the past, I guess. Dad and Mom take the whole business as seriously as he does, so I suppose they'll expect me to carry on the tradition someday. Another pebble in my boot.

Grampa came out of his office and beckoned Abby into the living room. I followed and stood in the doorway while he did something I'd seen him do a hundred times. He opened a drawer in the desk, hauled out a box, set it on the desk, and uncovered the old Bible, very carefully, as if it were made of ancient glass. As he laid his hand gently on its beat-up, powdery leather cover, the corners of his mouth twitched, sort of hinting a smile. "Here she is. The original. Half the pages are in pieces. But she's a beauty, isn't she?"

Abby nodded. "It's lovely," she whispered.

Grampa told her the story of the Bible. As he put it back in the drawer, he looked up. "I expect Paige will be taking care of this someday."

There it was again, the expecting.

Abby turned to me. Her eyes were shining. "Let's go, Paige. Show me Bible Corner."

I sighed. "Maybe some other time, Ab."

"My name's Abby, and if you'd rather not go, I'll find it by myself."

She never would find it. She'd probably get lost and wander around in circles and finally drop in a coma, and I'd be blamed. "You can't go alone. I'll have to take you, so come on."

Grampa chuckled. "If you're not back by dinner time, we'll get a search party going."

Fat chance we wouldn't be back before noon.

Out in the parking area by the barn, Dad, in his rubber jacket and trousers, was heading a sprayer tractor down the road. He waved as he passed us, and Abby waved back. "How come your dad's working on Saturday?"

"My dad works whenever he has to. This time of year he probably puts in a sixty-hour week at the least.

When apples need spraying and there's no wind, he sprays."

We walked around the barn, through grass and thistles and daisies, and into Tinker Field. The apples were still small on the trees. "These trees look like little old men standing in rows, don't they, Paige? They're all twisted and gnarled."

"I hadn't noticed."

"And I love the way they lean toward you as if they're telling you a secret. There's nothing nicer."

I could think of things that were nicer. Tall buildings with fast elevators and crowds of people talking and laughing and Cade Garrison in a good mood.

"You know what I like about being here?" Abby reached down and broke off a piece of grass and wound it around her finger.

"Can't imagine," I said, just to be moving my mouth.

"It's the quietness. The complete quietness."

"Spooky, isn't it?"

"I don't think it's spooky. I think it's exquisite."

Exquisite, for Pete's sake. Was she trying to impress me with those long, sappy words?

I had trouble finding the entrance to the path into the woods. Every year it gets overgrown. But after a couple of false starts, we were on our way. I let Abby go first so I could keep an eye on her. That crazy hat of hers kept getting knocked around by low branches. After a while she took it off, and as we moved along, the shadows and sunlight made specks on her dark hair. Actually she was a pretty good walker for a girl with skinny legs.

As she followed the path, she kept noticing things

and waving her hat around. "The ferns. Aren't they beautiful? They're nodding at us as if we're some kind of royalty."

She had a thing about royalty.

"Those fallen leaves, Paige. They're like a carpet under the trees."

I'd never paid much attention to fallen leaves, except when I slipped on wet ones.

"Did you know," she asked, "that the earth is made of fallen leaves and pine needles and wilted flowers?"

"And rotten apples."

"I love the smell of rotten apples."

"Do you have to love everything? Don't you ever hate anything?" There are so many things I hate, like kissing my cousins, and getting called on when I haven't done my homework.

"What was that rustle, Paige?"

It was probably a chipmunk popping out of its hole, but I said, "I expect it's a bear."

"Mm. Or maybe an Indian. There must have been Indians around here."

I hadn't got a rise out of her. Cade would have at least acted scared if I had mentioned bears, but Abby was tough to frighten. I was getting tired of her imagination, though.

"What's that way over there through the trees, Paige?" She was pointing to Laurabell's cabin. You could barely make out small gray sections of it. I was surprised Abby had spotted it.

"That's where Laurabell lives."

"Who's Laurabell?"

"She's an old woman who lives by herself." I told her

how Laurabell happened to be there. "You might have spotted her at church on Sunday." Laurabell sits at the back of the church. She's very old-fashioned about being black. "Don't want to go where I'm not wanted," she says. I keep telling her she's being silly, but she won't listen.

"I didn't see her," said Abby now. "Let's go visit her right away, Paige."

"Listen, do you want to see Laurabell or Bible Corner? Make up your mind, because we don't have time to do both."

"Oh, all right. We'll go to Bible Corner. But I want to meet Laurabell sometime. You've got to take me, Paige."

Did she think I was her personal full-time escort? "You can get there by yourself. Just take the path we were on the other day."

"But I don't even know her. I can't just walk in on her."

"You walked in on Grampa."

"Take me, Paige."

I shrugged.

"Good," she said.

She seemed to think a shrug meant yes. Well, all right. If I introduced her to Laurabell, she'd have someone to pester besides me.

We walked along in silence, with Abby chewing on her blade of grass. Finally she turned around and stared at me with those puddly eyes of hers. "Paige, are you frightened of your dad?"

"Sheez! Of course not."

"Then how come you won't let him know how you

feel about running the farm?"

"I told you. I don't want to hurt his or Mom's feelings. It's like walking a fence."

"That's only an excuse."

The problem with Dad had come on gradually over the years, so that until about a year ago I'd only suspected what he wanted from me. But since I'd been in high school, he'd made it clearer and clearer, until now there was no question. My staying had to be important to him, not only because someone had to take over, but because of the history of this place. One of our ancestors had brought apple seeds over from England, for pete's sake. How can you fight a thing like that?

Sometimes I think Dad loves this farm more than he loves any person, including me. He'll do anything for it that he has to. So maybe I *was* scared of him, of what he'd think of me if I told him. Maybe I was even a little bit of a coward. Maybe I thought that if I didn't talk to him about the problem, it would pick up and sneak away.

Abby and I were standing stock-still in the path glaring at each other. "You're pretty namby-pamby," she said. "Why don't you just face up to him and tell him?" She snapped her fingers. "Like that."

"Oh, sure. It sounds easy, doesn't it?"

"Right."

"Hey, I'd like to see you do the same kind of thing with your dad."

"I can't, you nincompoop. He's in Hong Kong." She swung around and marched ahead.

So I'm namby-pamby, am I? So I'm a nincompoop. I wished she'd trip and fall on that sharp chin of hers. I wished she'd break her pushy jaw.

"Are we almost there, Paige?"

"Won't be long." Thank goodness. I thought of the whole summer stretching before me, with Abby coming at me from all directions. "How come you're spending the summer here?" I asked her.

"My parents will be in Hong Kong the whole time. Dad's opening a branch office, with lots of entertaining, eating grasshoppers and eels and stuff. They didn't want me around."

No wonder.

Ahead of us were the tumbledown walls, with most of their rocks lying on the ground covered with weeds. There was the place where the walls came together, the corner where Grampa keeps the Bible in a space behind a couple of loose stones. Some of the stones near the top were missing. They'd probably fallen out and been picked up.

"This must be it," said Abby. "Isn't this exciting?"

"Yeah. Thrilling."

"You're being sarcastic, Paige."

I was. I was even being kind of repulsive. But I was still smarting from being called names. People don't usually do that to me.

Abby was all but flapping her arms like the wings of some butterfly, almost losing her balance. I had to hide a smile. "Show me, Paige. Where's it hidden?"

"Hey, take it easy. You'll have a stroke." I reached into the hole.

There was nothing there but empty air.

SEVEN

"It's not there, is it?" Abby had guessed, by looking at my face, that the Bible was missing.

I was more upset than I would have expected. "Maybe I'm looking in the wrong place." I took out more loose stones. I poked my hand all around. Nothing. "It's been stolen," I said. "Crummy trick, stealing a Bible."

"I'm sorry, Paige. I know how you feel. It's dreadful."

We inspected the ground, thinking the Bible might have fallen out, or even been blown away, but it wasn't there.

"Got to tell Grampa," I said.

We found him still in his office reading one of his farm journals. When I gave him the news, he shook his head and pulled at his lower lip. "It's a pity. Especially with Bibles costing so much nowadays. They're worth every penny, but they do run some high, and I only put that one in last October."

"Got an idea who could have taken it, Grampa? Who'd do a thing like that?"

"Well, now, you know how this place swarmed with

deer hunters last fall. You didn't dare so much as stick your head out the window. One of those chaps must have run across it and thought it was there for the taking."

"But those men have to get permission to hunt here. They know this is our property."

"Sure, it is. But whoever it was probably figured nobody cared about a Bible sitting in a pile of stones." He chuckled. "Ought to do him a deal of good, whoever he may be." He gave me a sharp look. "Quit your frowning, Paige. Nothing we can do about it."

That was probably true, but I was all the hotter because of it. What made me so mad, anyway? It was only a book.

For once Abby was quiet. When she and I parted out at the road to go home for noon dinner, her lip quivered and her eyes brimmed with tears. How come? It wasn't her Bible.

On Sundays Mom and Dad drag Joyce and me to church. Grampa goes with us and comes for dinner afterward.

That next morning, the five of us sat in the same pew with the Winches. After Harvey Biggs's mom had sung her solo and old Mr. Carver, behind us, had said to his wife in his bullhorn voice, "Myra Biggs's hat looks like the tractor ran over it," and after the giggles had broken out, and after Mrs. Biggs had given Mr. Carver a look that should have cut him in two, and after Harvey Biggs had shut his eyes and hunched his shoulders out of embarrassment, our minister, Mr. Pavlik, preached on the subject Thou Shalt Not Steal. "There are many ways of stealing," he said, shoving his glasses up his nose. But I had an idea that one of the meanest ways was to steal somebody's Bible.

I suppose a detective like Gibson might have figured out who stole it. But those deer hunters come from miles around, and lots of them are strangers to me. Earl Sanders hunts once in a while with his buddies. I'd put Joyce up to asking him a few questions.

As we came out of church, moving slowly on account of Grampa's arthritis, I caught up with Joyce. "Has Earl ever said anything to you about a Bible?"

She screwed up her face in a puzzled look. "A Bible? Earl?"

"Yeah. See, our Bible's missing from Bible Corner, and since Earl hunts some, I thought he or one of his friends might have, um, come on it."

She narrowed her eyes. "Paige Truitt, I think you've got the notion Earl stole that Bible."

"I never said—"

"No, but you implied. And I know for a fact that if he'd found it, he would have returned it. Earl Sanders is the dearest, straightest person there is, and I can't see why you're all against him. All of you." Her voice broke. She rushed to the car and scrambled into the front seat.

What had I said or done that was so awful? Earl hadn't been all that straight the time he'd wanted the BMW.

Cade was waving to me. She and her family had been chatting with Mr. Pavlik. She had on a yellow dress that swirled around her bare legs as she walked with the others toward the car. I thought of how she'd been at

Piney Pond yesterday, bossing people around, glowing with tan, laughing a lot, giving me flirty smiles. I thought of her softness when I kissed her.

"Who's that?" asked Abby, walking up behind me and taking my arm.

"Her name's Cade Garrison."

"She's exceptionally pretty."

"Mm."

"I never heard the name Cade before. I'll bet it came from some romantic book."

I didn't think the name was romantic. It was just a name. I examined Abby's face, thinking she must be kidding, but she looked perfectly serious. When I looked back at Cade, she was frowning. I quickly pulled my arm away from Abby as Cade turned her back. Was she upset? Did she think there was something between Abby and me? Abby, for pete's sake!

Abby nodded in the other direction. "Is that Laurabell?"

Laurabell was heading toward home. She always walked or biked. Wouldn't accept a ride. "Yup, that's Laurabell."

"Let's go talk to her."

I shrugged. "Why not?"

When we caught up, Abby said, "Hello, Laurabell. I'm Abby Winch. I'm staying with my grandparents, the Winches. Could Paige and I come to see you sometime?"

Laurabell, in her cotton shift and her tennis shoes, stood in the road with her feet apart and a murky smile breaking the lines of her face. "Sure, Abby. You come ahead."

"When? When shall we come?"

Laurabell chuckled. "Why, you come this afternoon, you're so anxious." She walked away slowly, breathing hard, shaking her head.

So I was in for it. Now I'd have to take her.

We went over on the three-wheeler, and right after we'd walked in the door, Abby began pestering Laurabell. "Paige won't tell me much about this place. I want to hear everything. What it's like in winter and all."

Laurabell smiled. "Snow drifts six feet high up against my door sometimes. That's what it's like in winter. But wait till spring, when the apple blossoms looks like stars in the sky, so many you can't count." She shook her head. "I tells you, it's worth all the aching and complaining."

Abby nodded eagerly. She and Laurabell were getting along fine, sitting at the table in the metal-and-Formica chairs. So what was I doing hanging around looking at the knots in the roof beams? It was boring hearing about the farm. I already knew about the farm, and they were talking as if it were the Promised Land. How can you get excited about things that are familiar to you, such a part of your life you barely notice them?

They're like margarine on bread, or clean sheets on Mondays.

On the Fourth of July, cousins come to the Hill from all around. I always think of those family picnics as some kind of contest to see who can bring the most food. As usual, my Uncle Howard and Aunt Pris drove up from south of Portland with my cousin Gary and with enough baked beans to feed the United States Navy. "I declare," said Aunt Pris, throwing her head back to look at me. "You're getting mighty tall, Paige. And that smile of yours is a pleasure. Bet the girls are flocking around."

My face went prickly. I was blushing again. Dad beamed. His hand fell onto my shoulder. "He's doing all right on the farm too, Pris. Good worker. Coming along nicely." Meaning, of course, that he was getting me ready to take over. Preparing me, the way you prepare a chicken before you broil it. I wish he wouldn't say things like that, especially in front of witnesses.

Uncle Howard is Dad's younger brother, who's an architect in Portland. He never had any interest in taking over the farm. Couldn't wait to get away. Makes me wish I had a brother who likes farming.

After we'd put the food into our stomachs, Grampa and Aunt Pris and some of the others watched the rest of us play baseball. As catcher, I'd just tagged Mom out at home when I noticed that Abby had come up the hill and was standing by the road watching us out of her deep-hole eyes. I hadn't seen that crazy hat of hers since our walk to Bible Corner, so she must have given up on it. Her face was sunburned, and I made out flecks of white on her nose where it had peeled. With her bangs nearly down to her eyebrows, she made me think of a stray orphan. "Hi, Paige," she called.

"Hi." She looked so forlorn I had to say it. "If you want to play, you can get out in the field."

She ran to where I was pointing, to just in front of Grampa's blueberry bushes, near where my cousin Gary was standing. She was our fourth fielder, but one more didn't make any difference.

Joyce, in the white shorts she'd finished sewing up yesterday, made the third out for the other team, striking three times while Noodles and Wiz chased each other around second base. "It's not fair," she said, giggling. "The dogs distracted me."

As the teams changed places, Gary chatted with Abby. He was thirteen, the same age she was, and about the same height. When they got near me, he was saying, "You'll be up third, Abby, right after me." So he already knew her name.

Dad got on base, Gary got on base, and it was Abby's turn. Standing with her legs apart, knees bent, gritting her teeth and holding the bat tightly behind her shoulders, she looked like some grasshopper. On the first pitch she plowed into that ball and hit a bullet of a grounder that skipped past people's legs and back, back, back into the blueberry bushes. Her eyebrows went up, and she stared in surprise. I found myself yelling, "Run, Abby!" She ran. Fast. Like some deer.

Dad crossed home plate first. When he turned and saw her circling the bases, he slapped his knee and roared with laughter. "Go, Abby, go!" Sheez! She'd hit a three-run homer. The Bartlett High football coach says I'll make first-string quarterback this fall, and I'd take her on as a fullback anytime. What speed!

As she crossed home plate, Gary was all over her, patting her on the back, calling out, "Way to go, Abby, way to go!" Just like a thirteen-year-old.

But as I watched Abby's excited face, a warmth went creeping up my neck.

* * *

The next day was Sunday, and that afternoon Cade's parents threw a lobster cookout, a fifteenth birthday party for her, out at Piney Pond. Even though it was cloudy and cool, just about everyone in next year's sophomore class was there. The place was crawling with swim trunks, bikinis, bare flesh, the smell of bug spray and suntan lotion, and Cade's brother Dennis. Cade put on her usual show with the wind-surfer, and after everyone else had got tired of taking it out, I had a chance to give Dennis another lesson. It wasn't long before he could surf by himself for a few minutes before we turned over. He was getting the feel of the thing nicely. When we came out, he was shivering in the chilly air. "Go on in, Dennis, and dry off, huh?"

"Okay," he said, running in the direction of the cabin. But halfway there, he turned and called out, "Thanks, Paige. Hey, thanks."

Cade, who was sitting with a group on the sand, said, "Mom'll be furious."

"She might as well get used to it." I pulled on my T-shirt, sat next to her, and watched the waves nipping at the edge of the pond. The sun was setting on the far side of the water, with the pines and birches eating into it bit by bit.

An hour or two ago, Cade's father had built a fire in the grill and set a big iron pot full of water on it. Now he came out of the cabin to add lobsters. When they were all in, and just before he fit the cover on, he looked in and said, "Comfy?" He's got this dry sense of humor. After a minute Mrs. Garrison turned up with an apron around her dumpy waist, carrying a bowl of tossed salad almost as big around as she was, and a basket of bread. She set them on the table.

All this time, Cade had been ignoring me, chatting with Rusty and some others. Now she turned to me. "I hear your cousin from Portland is some taken with Abby Winch."

Now, how had she heard about Gary's paying all that attention to Abby? He'd only met her yesterday, but probably Aunt Pris had been talking to her Bartlett relations. Everyone's connected with everyone. I hate the way news gets around our village so fast. If you as much as sneeze, everyone knows.

"Looks that way," I said. "But I doubt Gary can do much about it, with him living better than forty miles away."

"Can't imagine he'd want to. She looks puny to me."

"Puny! Hey, she hit a home run in our ball game. How come you're picking on her, for pete's sake?"

Cade gave me a quick look. "You do flare up wicked fast, Paige Truitt."

What was bugging her, anyway? I'd known her to be ugly to other people sometimes, but never to me. Except for once, last January, when we freshmen put on the play *Cinderella* for the grade-school kids and I was stage manager. Cade had the fairy godmother part, in a foamy blue-and-silver thing she'd worked on for a month, and I was supposed to surround her with clouds of steam blown from a dry-ice machine backstage. I couldn't see her from behind the curtain, and during her big scene I cranked out so much steam she was nearly blanked out from the audience. She'd snubbed me for a week.

But this time I hadn't done a thing.

Still, she warmed up to me later on. After she'd blown out the candles on her cake with lots of giggles, and after everyone had a piece on a paper plate, she kept feeding me bites of hers. "Here's one for good luck," she said, "even though it's not your birthday. And here's one to grow on."

I chuckled. "Yeah. If I eat this and mine too, I'll swell up like the Goodyear blimp."

"I don't care. You'd still be good-looking, you big dope." She smeared frosting on my face. So naturally I had to do the same thing to her, and we ended up in a crazy, wild frosting fight.

With Cade, you never know.

EIGHT

A couple of days later, Harvey and I were propped against trees in Ingram Field munching our lunch with the other workers. Harvey pulled up his socks so the tops were about six inches below the bottoms of his jeans, unwrapped his second ham sandwich, took a bite about a foot square, chewed it, and swallowed it. I could understand why he'd won the pie-eating contest at last summer's Bartlett Bicentennial Celebration.

He pointed the sandwich toward Huntville and started talking real estate. "Folks from Portland bought Old Lady Riddle's place over there." He shoved his cap back and leaned on an elbow. "Land's getting more and more valuable." Besides owning the village grocery with Harvey's mom, his dad is doing a great business in real estate. "Look at the way people are moving out from town in crowds," said Harvey, smiling into space. "And my dad's got something to sell them. I tell you, Paige, you're lucky your dad's an orchardist and you're going to have so much property."

"Sure. But what I'll have is farmland."

"Right. So you could sell it off in lots someday.

Wouldn't need to do a lick of work the rest of your life."

Somehow that idea gave me a lift, an electric feeling. But the feeling faded, I don't know why. It faded and disappeared. I thought of Dad and Mom, and Grampa puttering around his little house, building fires in the winter, keeping his account books. I thought of Laurabell, and the Winches. I thought of Bible Corner. And all the generations of people who had loved the Hill, who had worked to make it grow and produce.

Hey, what had got into me all of a sudden?

On Saturday, it was my turn to stop for hot dogs and potato chips at the grocery and to pick up Rusty and Harvey for Piney Pond. Mom never lets me borrow the Chevy Nova without saying, "You take it easy, now. Any numskull can shove a foot on the accelerator. It takes brains to take care and stay alive."

She said it this time.

As I got to where our road hits the Bartlett Road, I saw Abby up ahead, walking to the village with a shopping bag, so naturally I slammed on the brakes and skidded to a stop opposite her. "Want a ride?"

She didn't waste any time getting into the car. "Thanks. Where you going?"

"Over to Piney Pond. The Garrisons spend weekends there summers, and on Saturday afternoons we go over and mess around."

"Who's we? The big shots from your high school class?"

"Come on, Abby, we're not all that big." She was probably right, though. Now that she'd brought up the idea, I had to tell myself that in a couple of years we'd probably be running the school. But how had Abby figured that out? Was there something about me that told her? Was there something about Cade?

I changed the subject. "So how come you're walking to town, huh?"

"Well, see, Grandmother's on one of her pie-baking sprees, and she's getting low on flour. Grandfather's off in the car somewhere, so I thought I might as well get some exercise and walk to the store, it's such an enchanting day."

Enchanting. Sheez!

The Garrisons' red Volvo was parked outside the grocery. Maybe Cade's dad or mom had come over from Piney Pond to see Mr. Biggs or to do an errand. As we climbed the wooden stairs, Abby whispered, "Does Mrs. Biggs wear that weird hat in the store?"

I grinned. "Nope. Only her false teeth."

Abby giggled so hard that the person standing at the counter talking to Mrs. Biggs turned and stared. It was Cade.

I wiped the grin off my face. "Hello. Thought you'd be at the pond."

She frowned. "Well, I'm not. I'm stocking up."

Mrs. Biggs was taking cans and jars from the counter and putting them into paper sacks. Those sacks would be heavy. "Can I help carry things?" I asked Cade.

"No, thanks. I'll do it." Her voice was cold.

"I'm Abby Winch," said Abby Winch.

Cade's smile seemed pasted on. "I'm Cade Garrison. I heard the Winches' young granddaughter was here." She emphasized the word *young*.

"I love it here," said Abby. "It's magnificent. Paige and I are planning to climb a mountain, aren't we, Paige? And I'll bet Piney Pond is exquisite." She ran out of breath.

Cade's eyebrows moved up a fourth of an inch. "It's nice," she said. "Maybe Paige will show you his snapshots sometime." She picked up her groceries, one heavy sack in each arm, gritted her teeth, and marched out of the store.

Sure, Abby had been half asking for an invitation to Piney Pond, but Cade hadn't needed to be so ugly to her. And sure, Cade and I had paired off for years. But was the sight of me with another girl that hard for her to take?

Abby took off for home with her ten-pound bag of flour in the shopping bag. "Can you manage it all right?" I asked as she walked out the door lopsided.

"I'll be fine, Paige. Perfectly fine."

I turned to Mrs. Biggs, who smiled so I could see her straight white teeth. "Everyone all right up to the Hill?" she asked. "Haven't seen Laurabell. She hasn't been in all week."

"We're all okay, thanks. Say, it's my turn to bring hot dogs and potato chips to the pond today. Think I should take crinkled instead of plain for a change?" Mrs. Biggs always likes to be consulted.

"Well, I'll tell you, Paige, I know my Harvey likes his potato chips plain. No need to get fancy with him." She shook her head. "Sometimes I think that boy's got a hollow leg. Where does he put all the stuff he eats? Lucky me and his dad have got this store." She leaned on the counter, ready for conversation.

"Well," I said quickly, "I'd better get moving. I'll settle for the same old thing, then. Got to pick up Harvey and the others in five minutes." I rounded up the food and plunked it on the counter. That got her moving.

When I went out to the car, I got a last look at Abby, struggling along with the shopping bag nearly scraping the road.

Out at Piney Pond, Cade said, "Hi, lover boy."

"What's this lover boy stuff?"

"Aren't you one? You were all over that girl. The one who talks like an encyclopedia."

"I was not all over her."

"Well, you seemed to be having an awfully good time with her."

"Is there some federal regulation against having a good time?"

"Hmp." Cade stuck her nose in the air and turned away.

How could she be jealous of Abby? Abby was only thirteen.

Later on, when I finally got Cade alone, I figured she must have forgotten about Abby. When I kissed her, she smiled and said, "Mmm." Her voice came out low and sweet and innocent. She leaned on my arm and looked out over the lake. "Paige, you're not really going to take that girl Abby mountain climbing."

"Sure, I am. She's new here. She wants to see things. Hey, it's only Scrubtop. It's not the Appalachian Trail, for pete's sake."

"I think you could show a little loyalty to me."

"Look, Cade, I am loyal to you. Okay. So Abby

sweet-talked me into taking her up that mountain. Big deal. Look, I'm not going to *marry* her."

"I don't want you to do it, Paige."

That burned me. I wasn't exactly dying to take Abby up Scrubtop, but I wasn't going to have Cade ordering me around. "Well, I'm going to."

Cade sat up straight. "Go ahead and spoil our fun. All right for you, Paige Truitt." She got up and walked away, leaving me disgusted. I never knew she could turn from hot to cold so fast. She didn't make sense.

Before church the next day, Abby sat down next to me in the pew and whispered questions in my ear. "Who's the bald man over there?" It was Mr. Biggs, Harvey's dad. "Is that Harvey next to him?" It was. "Well, what about Mr. Pavlik, the minister? Is he married?" Yes, he was, and he had two young daughters, and would she please shut up. She shut up.

After the service, the Garrisons followed the Winches and Truitts down the steps. I felt someone poke me between my back ribs and turned to see it was Dennis. "Hiya, Paige." He grinned. "When do I get another surfing lesson?"

I glanced at Mrs. Garrison. "That depends on what your parents say."

Mr. Garrison shoved his suit jacket back and rested his thumbs under his suspenders. "Any time, Paige."

"Do you really think he should?" asked Mrs. Garrison, looking worried.

"He's safe with Paige," said Mr. Garrison.

"Oh, I'm sure of that." She gave me a warm smile.

Even though she's a worrywart, she and I always get along.

Abby chose this time to introduce herself. "I'm Abby Winch," she said. "You must be Mr. and Mrs. Garrison, and I'm charmed to meet you."

Cade had been standing motionless, with no expression. Now she brushed past us and swished down the sidewalk without opening her mouth. Well, if she had to clam up like some jealous nut, that was her problem.

On the way home, Mom said, "Did you notice that Laurabell wasn't in church? Do you suppose she's ailing?"

I spoke up. "Mrs. Biggs said she didn't come in for provisions all week."

"Hm. Maybe she took a chill. Best I boil up my chicken bones after dinner and send over some broth with you, Paige."

"Can't do it, Mom. Rusty's coming over."

"Rusty can wait," said Dad. "Time you learned that we Truitts take care of our own."

"But Laurabell's about as helpless as a bear."

"All of us are helpless sometimes. Could be she is now. Anyway, Paige, it won't take you more than a few minutes."

I was stuck. I never did mind going to Laurabell's, but I hated having my day interrupted. She was probably fine. I wished she had a phone so Mom could call her and check.

We had Mom's blueberry pie for dinner, served on the good dessert plates. When Dad finished, he set his fork down and said, "Got to go check the Macs over to Butterworth."

Mom shook her head. "Ned, I declare you never stop. You treat those apples like your own children."

Dad chuckled. "Well, Lou, I'd never sell my own children." The smile disappeared. He sat playing with his fork, turning it over and over. "Lou, you've got to remember I grew up with this place. I've seen how it grows and changes, and how it stays the same. Always the same." He stared at the fork. His eyes were damp.

"I know, Ned." Mom's words reached out to him across the table. "I know."

No one said a word.

After a minute Dad swallowed, cleared his throat, picked up his napkin, wiped his whole face, pushed his chair back, and clumped out the door.

I watched him as he crossed the yard.

How could I tell him? How could I ever tell him?

Naturally, Noodles barked as I rode the three-wheeler down the road past the Winches' with Mom's plastic soup container in the basket. So naturally Abby rushed out onto the porch. Her sunburn had become a tan that took away the ready-to-break look she'd had earlier. Her bangs reached her eyebrows now. She looked like a new puppy. "Where you going, Paige?" she hollered over the noise of the engine.

That girl had more questions than any game show.

I stopped and told her. She shoved her bangs to one side. I wished she'd show some sense and cut them. "I'll come with you," she said. "I like Laurabell. She's so character-faced."

Character-faced. Good grief! I looked at the sky, and then I looked at her. "Why don't you cut your bangs?"

"Because I'd get them crooked. Don't change the subject, Paige. Take me."

I sighed. "Okay, hop on," I said, to shut her up.

She hopped on. Before I could kick into gear, she asked, "Is Cade mad at you?"

I shrugged. "Maybe."

"I think she's a snot."

"You be careful what you say about Cade." I was beginning to feel caught in some kind of crossfire.

"I will not be careful. I'll bet lots of people say nasty things about her. The wimps, I mean. The kids in your school who aren't all that popular. You're one of the popular ones, so you wouldn't know. Anyway, I feel sorry for her."

"She doesn't need your sympathy. She can take care of herself."

"Can she?"

What made her think she knew so much? She made me mad. I pressed the accelerator and took off.

Laurabell wasn't out in her garden, where there were a few weeds growing between the rows of vegetables. I was still parking the three-wheeler when Abby marched up the steps between the marigold beds to the battered front door and gave a sharp knock. Callie's mewing came from inside, and then the low murmur of Laurabell's voice. Abby creaked the door open and disappeared. When I caught up with her, bringing the soup, I found that she and Callie had gone through the room that served as a living room and kitchen and into the bedroom. Laurabell was sick, all right. She lay in her bed in a thin cotton nightie with her head bent up onto the pillow, gazing at us from the shadows. The outline of her body showed through the skimpy sheet.

Callie jumped onto the bed and lay next to her feet. "I think it's disgraceful," Abby was saying in her fuzzy voice. "It's awful, the way you've been neglected."

I was about to flare up and speak when Laurabell spoke instead. "Nobody neglects me, girl. Truitts have been a comfort to me for more time than you've been alive. Besides, they don't owe me nothing. I takes care of myself, and I keeps my self-respect. If I didn't have that, I might as well be dead." She shook her head. "Nope. I never wanted for anything I truly needed. Never asked for anything I didn't."

Abby bit her lip. Laurabell examined her out of the whiteness of her eyes, her breath coming in puffs, her skin stretched over her cheekbones. Had I just not noticed those things before, or had they come on suddenly? This was a whole new Laurabell. She made me feel shaky, unsure of myself. The kidding business wouldn't work today.

She coughed.

"Laurabell," said Abby, "you ought to go to the hospital."

"Don't believe in hospitals. People dies in hospitals."

"Well, you should at least see the doctor."

"Saw him last year when my wrist broke, and he hammered and poked me in places nobody ought to mention in public. For a busted wrist. Shoot!" She went into a coughing fit I thought would go on forever. The veins in her neck popped out. Her fingers, in front of her face, looked like claws. I felt sick and helpless. Abby clenched her teeth.

Back when Mom had driven Laurabell to town with her broken wrist, she'd secretly asked the doctor to give her a physical.

Finally Laurabell's coughing stopped. Her shoulders heaved, and her breath came in puffs again. "Been trying to take it easy. Most times I lies here and reads my Bible, but sometimes Callie and I likes to go out and watch the sunset."

"In San Antonio," said Abby quietly, "it's hard to see the sunset. Too many tall buildings." She shook her bangs away from her eyes and gave Laurabell a long look. "How much food have you got?"

Laurabell considered. "I got enough to last me a while. This and that."

"We brought you some, didn't we, Paige?"

I finally found my tongue. "Some of Mom's chicken broth." I held up the container.

Laurabell gave me a thin smile. "Your mom cooks up elegant broth. Makes my mouth water and my stomach purr." She gave a low cackle that ended in a cough.

"Go heat some up, Paige." Abby, the thirteen-year-old, was giving me orders.

In the outer room, Callie's food dish was tipped over on the floor. There were dishes in the sink sticky with egg and peanut butter. I checked out the fridge. There was a one-quart milk carton that looked about a third full. There were two eggs, and three slices of bread in a plastic bag. In the food cupboard were a jar of peanut butter and some home-preserved vegetables.

I got out a saucepan, poured it half full of soup, turned on a burner, and set the soup on the stove. It did look good, with bits of carrots and potatoes and parsley floating in it. While I waited for the soup to heat, I looked closely at the only picture on the wall, an enlarged snapshot of Billy and Laurabell on their wedding day in Mississippi. Billy was laughing down at her. She looked about Joyce's age, slim in a short white dress and sandals, with long hair blown back by a breeze.

When I came back into the bedroom with the soup, the pillow behind Laurabell had been plumped, and Abby was smoothing the sheet. She stepped aside while I put the bowl into Laurabell's bony fingers. Laurabell grasped it and shoveled spoonfuls into her mouth as fast as she could. Abby stood at the foot of her bed fondling Callie, but watching Laurabell and nodding, as if she were forcing the soup down into Laurabell's stomach with her chin. When Laurabell had finished every drop, Abby said, "Want some more?"

Laurabell shook her head, breathing hard, the way you do when you've run a race. Her eyelids drooped. "I'm weary," she said with a faint smile. "I'll sleep now, thank you kindly."

Abby passed me and moved to the head of the bed. "I'll get your pillow down."

Laurabell shook her head. "Leave it be, Miss Abby. I does better with my head up." She chuckled. "Always did."

"All right, Laurabell." Abby tucked in the sheet. "Paige, I saw lettuce in the garden. Go pick some."

More orders. When I brought the lettuce in, Abby had done the dishes. She washed the lettuce and rolled it in a towel and set it in the fridge. She found a bag of cat food, and poured some into Callie's dish, and set the dish back on the floor. "I'll be back tomorrow," she called to Laurabell. But Laurabell hadn't heard. She was asleep.

NINE

When I let Abby off, she asked, "How does Laurabell stay warm on cold nights?"

"Didn't you see that old iron stove in the main room? She kept it when she got the electric one. The men bring her sticks for it when they clear out the woods. There's a pile out back."

"And that stove keeps her warm?"

"Warm as toast."

She raised her eyebrows. She didn't believe me. But I'd told her the truth.

Mom called the doctor in Milton, told him about Laurabell's stubbornness, and got him to prescribe an antibiotic. "He says it may be pneumonia," she said. "I'll drop off the pills and talk her into going into the hospital. She can't stay in that place."

But she did. Mom, with that no-funny-business way of hers, couldn't even persuade her to come up to the Big House. It's a tradition in our family that anyone close to us who's sick or orphaned or in other trouble stays at the Big House. But Laurabell wouldn't think of coming. She was too proud, I guess.

Mom and Mrs. Winch started taking turns making nourishing soups and stews for Laurabell, who couldn't stop them from doing it. And Abby would take them to her, walking down the woods path. Abby would stay and clean house, wash dishes, feed Callie, freshen the sheets, help Laurabell to the bathroom and to her meals, weed the garden. She even rigged up foil tins on sticks to blow in the wind and scare animals away from the vegetables. Some days, when it got chilly, she'd start the wood stove.

Mom said Abby was a marvel. I guess she was right.

After work on a cool, cloudy day late in the week, Thursday as I recall, I was driving the Chevy Nova from the farm the twelve miles to Milton to pick up my developed pictures, some film, and garden tools for Mom. Wiz had wanted to come, so I let him in the back seat and told him to behave himself. As I took off, Abby was coming out of Puckett Field, through the daisies and clover, toward the road. She was on her way back from Laurabell's carrying a wad of soiled, patched sheets as big as she was. Against the chill, she'd put on a sweater, an expensive-looking pink-and-blue cardigan that hung almost to her knees. She looked tired.

I stopped the car. "How's Laurabell?" I asked.

Abby shook her head. "She doesn't have any energy. You'd think she'd be getting her strength back, with all that nourishing food and the pills, but she's not. And she's coughing lots more."

A chill went through me. I wondered about Laurabell's age. Was she sixty? Seventy? Eighty? Maybe even ninety or a hundred? I'd never stopped to think.

"Where are you going, Paige?"

I told her.

"I'll go too."

She'd been working hard the last few days. She looked used up, and tight. A drive might help her relax. "Okay. Should you check with your grandparents?"

"I don't think they're home yet. I'll leave a note."

She was back in a moment without the laundry, and she hopped in beside me. "That's some sweater," I said.

"Thanks. Mom gave it to me. She was tired of it."

As I took the curve at the south woods, I said, "I wish Laurabell would show some sense and come to the Big House." Of course I admired her independence, but now she was worse, and there was no point in her being foolish. There was smoke from her chimney coming out of the clearing to our left. Abby had started the stove, but what would have happened if Abby hadn't gone there?

"But she loves the cabin," Abby said. "Can't you understand about loving a place? Like this farm. Don't you care about it?"

I wrinkled my nose. "I never thought there was anything so awfully special about here. It's just an old farm in the country."

"What a revolting thing to say! Anyway, how do you know it would help if Laurabell left her place? When old people give up their homes, it takes a great deal out of them. Don't you even know that?"

It was time I straightened her out. "Abby, you're a good kid. I'm getting to like you. But you've got to get over your superiority complex. What makes you think, for instance, that we Truitts are neglecting Laurabell?"

"I didn't say you Truitts in particular."

"Yeah? Well, that's what you meant. And if you knew anything about it, you'd know we've done everything we can for Laurabell, and that she's as stubborn as a Guernsey heifer about accepting things. You don't know everything, so quit pretending you do."

She was quiet. Finally she spoke in a small, strangled voice. "I don't think I know everything. I don't think I know anything much. Actually I feel pretty stupid."

"You certainly take a funny way of showing it."

She sniffled. I'd pushed too far. I'd been mean. "Hey, I'm sorry."

Silence.

Out of the corner of my eye I saw her arm come up. She wiped her face on the sleeve of her mother's pink-and-blue cardigan. She took a deep breath and said, letting the breath out in little gasps, "I guess I've got into the habit. See, one way I can get my parents' attention is to act very, very intelligent. Otherwise they don't notice me unless they're in the mood." She was talking louder now, and faster, like a motorboat picking up speed. "I don't know why I'm telling you this. I mean, because you wouldn't understand what it's like. People always pay attention to you."

"I paid attention to you at Laurabell's the other day."

"That was different. That was an emergency."

"You did all right." That was as far as I was ready to go toward admitting she had outshone me where Laurabell was concerned.

At the crossroads in the village, the Garrisons' Volvo was turning north onto the main road with Mrs. Garrison and Cade in the front seat. We waved but Cade gave us a hard look and didn't wave back. Something twisted inside me.

Sheez! I hadn't realized how cold she can be when she turns you off. Or how it feels.

Abby said, "Has she been snubbing you a lot?"

"Yup. I don't care, though." I made a quick decision. "I'm not going to Piney Pond Saturday. Maybe I never will. Those guys are a bunch of babies."

She giggled. "Sure. And you're practically an adult."

"More of one than they are."

"So if you're not going, we can climb that mountain on Saturday."

I'd left myself wide open. I had no excuse not to. But in spite of Cade's weird attitude, I'd miss going to the pond and seeing her. Shoot! Why had I said what I'd said? "What about Laurabell?" I asked. "She'll need doing for."

"I'll do for her ahead of time. And I'll bring a picnic. Grandmother's got chicken in the freezer. You like her baked chicken?"

There's nothing I go for more than Mrs. Winch's baked chicken. We decided I'd try to get the Nova again and pick her up at nine in the morning after she'd been to Laurabell's.

We did the errands and headed back. The sky was darker than ever as we came up to the Exxon station on the edge of Bartlett. "I'm going to stop and see if Earl's still here," I said.

"Do we need gas?"

"Nope. Anyway, there's gas at home." I resisted the temptation to remind her that our pump was out in the yard by the mechanics' shop where she must have seen it. This wasn't the time to rub stuff in. I said, "I've been wanting to talk to him, that's all." I pulled up in front of the open door to the Exxon garage, behind Earl's rear end. He was working on Mr. Moreau's appliance repair van, with his head and his big shoulders under the open hood. "Hey, Sanders," I yelled.

He lifted his head, turned, and flashed me a grin that showed where those two teeth were missing. "Hey there, Truitt." Carrying a wrench, he lumbered over and plunked his elbows on the sill of my window, ready for a talk.

"How's it going?" I asked.

"Oh, round and round." As if he were illustrating his point, he twirled the wrench in his greasy hands. "How's Joyce?"

Since he'd been up at our place every night that week, I didn't think he needed to know. But I guess just talking about Joyce made him feel closer to her. "She was fine at breakfast," I said. "You know Abby Winch here?"

"Seen her around. Hi, Abby."

Abby smiled and nodded. Earl reached past me into the back seat to pat Wiz's nose. "You okay, Wiz?" he said softly. "They treating you right?"

I cleared my throat. "Say, Earl, you got any idea who might have been hunting last fall in the woods over beyond Tinker Field?"

He gave a low whistle. "Could have been anybody. We was all over that way. Why are you asking?"

A cream-colored Skylark with a New York license plate pulled into the station, and the bell rang inside the office. Mr. English, Stacey's grandfather, who owns the station, stepped through the scuffed office door with his gray hair flying every which way. Mr. English limps a little on account of his arthritis, but he moves fast. He rushed over to the Skylark, started the gas pumping, and began wiping the windshield, remarking to the young couple inside that, yes, it certainly did seem we were due for some mighty heavy rain, and it was a pity. He kept up the conversation, bobbing his head as he moved around washing the windows.

As I turned back to Earl, there was a roll of thunder. "I just wondered," I said. "The Bible's missing from Bible Corner. Ever heard the Bible Corner story?"

"Joyce told me something. Had to do with a boundary line."

"Yup. Well, I thought you might have seen somebody pick it up without knowing. It's of no importance except for the page out of the old Bible that Grampa stuck inside it."

Earl scratched his head with the wrench. "No way did I see that Bible. Hey, I'm sorry, Paige."

"That's okay. Look, I'd just as soon you didn't tell Joyce I asked you. I wanted her to ask, but that bothered her. She thought I was accusing you. You know I wouldn't do that, Earl." I shot him a grin.

He gave me a shove on the shoulder with his left hand, leaving some grease on my windbreaker. "Sure, Paige. I know how she gets sometimes." His voice was gentle, and his eyes were soft. "Anyways, I won't say nothing. And if I hear talk about a Bible, I'll pass you the word."

"Thanks, Earl."

I figure you can tell, just by looking, whether a per-

son is lying. I stared into Earl's eyes. They were return-
ing my look, as blue and clear as eyes can be. Earl
Sanders may not be the most ambitious person around,
but I made up my mind then and there that he's honest.

"The turnoff's about eight, nine miles north," Mr.
English was saying to the couple on vacation from New
York State. "Just past Tuckers' well-digging place." He
waved them goodbye and hustled over to talk to us.
"Howdy," he said. "Truitts all in good health?"

"Fine, thanks, Mr. English."

He turned to Earl. "You're working overtime, Earl.
How you coming with Joe Moreau's van?"

Earl lifted his elbows from my windowsill. "It's the
carburetor, Mr. English. I'm about done."

Mr. English turned to me. "I declare, that Earl
Sanders knows his autos. When he's working on an engine, he's a pleasure to watch."

Earl suddenly got interested in a stone next to his
left boot. I wondered if Dad hadn't passed up a good
bet when he had turned him down for a job in our
mechanics' shop.

Mr. English rambled on. "We're getting more customers now that Earl's here. Been trying to get him to
take over this station. Son won't do it. He's tied up at
the lumberyard. And my arthritis is some bad, especially in the hands. Wiping those windshields is a
chore." He gave a drawn-out sigh, half shutting his
eyes.

The station isn't much. Most of the summer people
fill up at the newer places in Milton. The office here
hasn't been painted in years. Mr. English must be a

tired man in spite of the obliging way he serves his customers.

Earl was kicking the stone back and forth. "Golly, Mr. English, I'm no manager. I don't take to all that paperwork. It don't interest me. Heck, I just want to fool around with motors."

I wondered how much money a good mechanic gets paid. If I had listened to Dad and asked questions, I'd know what they made at the farm. If Joyce married Earl, she'd be living on mechanics' wages, plus anything she could earn. Being Joyce, she'd want children. They'd never be rich, that was certain.

There was a flash of lightning, a growl of thunder, a spattering of raindrops. "Better get going," I said, twisting the ignition key. I turned on my lights and wiper and rolled up the window against the chill. I put the Nova into reverse and took off, waving.

As we started down the road again, I said to Abby, "You won't tell that I asked him about the Bible, will you?"

"Of course not."

"I didn't think you would."

By the time we got to the turnoff in the village, the rain was acting like a car wash, and there was hail mixed with the splashy drops. I was getting uptight. Hail's bad news on an apple farm. While it pounded our doors and windows, I pressed hard on the accelerator.

"Paige, you're going too fast." Abby's voice trembled.

"We've got to get back. This stuff can bruise the apples so they're spoiled for anything but cider."

"Oh, golly! Hey, I'm sorry, Paige. What can you do about it?"

"Nothing."

"Then why hurry? You can hardly see where you're going."

"I know, but I can't help it. I just feel I ought to be there. Dad'll be worried."

"Have you got insurance?"

I shook my head. "Dad says it doesn't pay. He's self-insured. He puts money in a pot, or something like that. But this could drain the pot, and then some."

"It's a shame. After all the work he's done. After the work you've all done. Not to mention the money. I know, Paige. I can understand."

Maybe she did. Maybe she really did.

TEN

We were in a pocket where there was no hail. Only drops of moisture on the windshield. Hail's like that. It comes in patches. I only hoped it was missing most of our place. But farther along we hit its clatter again, and it came, on and off, on and off, all the way back. As we turned onto the farm road, the car skidded. Abby gasped. But I managed to hold the wheel steady while the hail hit us full force. Off to our right, the smoke from Laurabell's cabin was being blown every which way. We clattered across the creek bridge and hurried up the hill past Butterworth Field. I had glimpses of trees fighting the wind, leaves swirling in waves, apples swaying.

I felt cold and clammy. Tears gushed into my eyes.

Why did I care so much?

Halfway up the hill, the hail disappeared, and when I stopped to let Abby off, there was only rain. I didn't turn my head. I hoped she wouldn't notice my soppy eyes.

She took my arm tightly in both of her hands and pressed her face against it for a minute. When she let go, she opened the door and scampered out into the rain, holding her sweater over her head. She hadn't said a word, but a glow seeped through me, as if I'd eaten some of Mom's hot soup.

At home, Mom was in the kitchen making noises with pots and pans. Joyce hummed as she set the table for supper. Dad sat at his desk, absolutely motionless, staring out at the storm. "Any news, Dad?"

He shook his head.

"Butterworth looks bad," I said, "but I think the old farm around Winches' is okay."

I had the feeling the worst was over. Afterward, he'd want to go out and check each field. I hoped the darkness wouldn't hinder him.

The rain slowed to a drizzle. Dad picked up the phone and dialed. "Amos?" That would be Amos Perry, whose apples Dad had contracted to pick and market. "Did you get hit?... About half, huh?... Well, don't you fret, Amos. I'll take 'em all. We'll truck the bruised ones over here and put 'em to cider.... No, Amos. It's all right. We made a deal." He hung up.

Mom had come to the kitchen doorway, wiping her hands on her apron. Joyce stood still, a glass in her hand. "Dad, if he's got all those bruised apples, that ought to be his problem, not yours."

"We made a deal," Dad repeated. Slowly he heaved himself up, crossed to the hall closet, and took out his slicker. "Come on, son," he said, "let's go check the damage."

Most of the Macs in Butterworth would have to go for cider. So would the Lodi in Ingram Field, where

Harvey and the others and I had slaved so hard. Otherwise there were only small sections of the orchards where there was damage. "Took about a fourth of our crop," said Dad, rubbing the stubble on his chin, "and half of Amos Perry's."

As usual, Joyce was cheerful. "It's all right, Dad. I've definitely made up my mind not to go to college, so you won't have that expense." He just stared at her. Had she decided to marry Earl? I guess Dad didn't know whether to be glad or sorry. There was no way I could tell him now that I didn't want to run the farm. He was worried about Joyce and upset about the storm.

At the church potluck supper the next evening, everyone talked about the storm. Mr. Garrison, who keeps some apple trees along with his dairy cows, had lost a third of his crop. "That was some wind," he said, stretching his suspenders. "Could've spit in my own eye." The Moreaus' oak tree had toppled onto their garage and bashed in the roof and the top of Mr. Moreau's service van. The plate-glass window at Mr. English's Exxon station had been smashed. When people asked Dad about his damage, he just shrugged his big shoulders and said, "We lost a few." I guess he couldn't bring himself to fuss about his troubles when others had some that were just as tough on them. Maybe tougher.

I guess everyone wanted to talk over the storm, because there was an overflow crowd, so some of us guys got pushed into setting up more chairs. As we worked, Rusty said to me, "I hear you went and got Cade's mom mad at you."

"Mrs. Garrison? Oh, come on, you old dustbag, she's crazy about me."

He opened a chair with a clatter. "Well, I heard you were on the outs with her on account of the way you've been trying to take over Dennis."

"Me? Take over Dennis?"

"You know. Getting him onto the surfer and all that dangerous stuff."

"Come off it, Rusty. Who's been feeding you that crop of fairy tales?" He shrugged and grabbed another chair. "Was it Cade?" I asked.

"Mm, well, um, everyone's talking about it. I heard Dennis is mad at you too."

It was Cade all right.

"Rusty," I said, "I never heard such a bunch of bull. With you spreading it around, it's going to be all over the county. You've got such fantastic vocal cords you ought to will them to science."

So Cade had been starting rumors. Cade, who had been my girl.

When it was time to pick up our food, we quit milling around in small groups and formed two lines, one on each side of the string of buffet tables. I was three people in front of Abby in one line. Cade, in a splashy silk print shirt and orange pants, was in line across from us, opposite Abby. When Abby got to Mom's cheese and lemon Jell-O mold, she squealed. "Ooh golly, what's this? It looks absolutely bewitching."

Cade rolled her eyes. "In that case," she said in her stage voice, "a witchy girl like you ought to love it."

There was silence as people looked and then pretended not to be looking. Abby turned red and ducked her head. I flipped. I mean, I was really sore. Shooting off sparks.

I waited till Cade filled her plate and began to wind her way through the crowd toward her table. I went up behind her.

"You lay off Abby," I said between my teeth. "Just lay off."

She lifted her chin and stared at me, hard. Her eyes burned. She'd always looked extra pretty when she was miffed, but she'd never looked at me that way except after *Cinderella*. In a quick flash, I thought of the years we'd been close to each other. I thought of tag games on the school playground when each of us would chase the other, and the funny notes we passed across the classrooms, and the way her smile had always left me kind of breathless. Thinking those things made me even madder.

Cade said, "I'll say whatever I want to say, Paige Truitt."

"Not to Abby, you won't. You stay away from her."

"I'd be delighted, she's such a wimp."

That did it. The magic between us had fizzled. Disappeared. Died. As she turned to go, I bumped her, and she went down. Her plate broke. Chicken, baked beans, corn bread, and Jell-O mold spread over the floor in a slimy mess.

There were gasps. People stopped. Things got quiet. Mr. Moreau leaned over Cade. "You all right, dear?"

She sat up looking dazed, wiping her face with her hand. There was food down the front of her shirt and pants. Mrs. Moreau knelt in front of her. "Can I help you up, Cade?" Mrs. Biggs ran to the kitchen for a mop. Mrs. Pavlik picked up pieces of plate. I wasn't needed. I split and headed for my table.

The thing that had blown me away was that she'd called Abby a wimp.

Except last fall, when Cade was running for class vice-president, she'd never been nice to the wimps in our class. How come I'd never noticed her meanness? Not till she was mean to Abby.

When I sat down next to Joyce, she said, "Honestly, Paige! Couldn't you have helped Cade? Didn't you see her fall?"

"She had plenty of help." I picked up the thigh from Mrs. Winch's baked chicken that I had on my plate and dug in.

I'd had enough of Cade Garrison.

After dinner, Joyce went off with Earl. I could see the members of my crowd gathering to go somewhere, Cade with food spots down the front of her clothes, Rusty chattering away, Harvey guffawing into Cade's ear. She was giving Harvey the flirty smile she'd always saved for me. I felt sort of sick. But nobody asked me to join them, and I didn't. Always before I'd been one of the ringleaders. I tried to tell myself I didn't care that I wasn't included, that the rumors they were spreading couldn't hurt me, but my throat felt tight. I was really spooked. After all the fun we'd had over the years, how could they ignore me that way?

As they left, Cade shot me a look full of hate. I had a feeling it wouldn't be long before the whole crowd knew why she'd fallen.

Mom drew her eyebrows together in a puzzled look. "Aren't you going off with your friends, Paige?"

"Nope."

"What happened, honey? Something must have happened."

"Nothing much."

"Tell me, Paige."

"Mom, will you quit bugging me?"

She shook her head. "Well, whatever it is, it's sure to blow over. I'm certain you'll work it out, Paige."

She had more faith in me than I did.

Mom had some leftover Jell-O mold she wanted to drop off at Laurabell's. "Maybe I could even coax her up to the Big House," she said, "though heaven knows I've tried before."

The cabin light was on, and I went in behind Mom and Dad, with Callie welcoming us at the door. Laurabell, in her skimpy nightie, sat at the little table by the wood stove lingering over a cup of something hot. She looked like a skeleton, with eyes that seemed to take up half her face, and hands like spiders. No wonder Abby was worried.

Callie lay down at Laurabell's feet, guarding her mistress.

Mom was all heartiness. "We brought you something, Laurabell. Have you got space left in your stomach?"

Laurabell tried to smile. "Well, I declare," she croaked. "Look at this. You know I loves your Jell-O mold, ma'am. It tingles my mouth."

"Can you eat it now, Laurabell?"

"Better you leave it."

The weariness showed in her voice. She started to push herself up from the table, but Mom put her hand on her arm. "Never mind, Laurabell, I'll take care of it." Laurabell plopped back into her chair and began to cough, while Mom stowed the mold in the fridge and Dad and I stared at the floor. When Laurabell had stopped coughing and had taken a sip from her cup, Mom said, "Laurabell, have you been taking your pills?"

"I surely has, ma'am. Miss Abby, she sees to it."

Mom picked up the medicine bottle from the table. "You'll need more. I'll get you some. And we're going to take you home with us right now. I'll pack your things." She bustled toward the bedroom.

There was a sudden gleam in Laurabell's eyes. She lifted her chin. She watched Mom's firm steps, Dad's serious expression, and what I hoped was my welcoming face, willing her to come. I was sure she would. She had to.

She looked around the little room. At the crewel pillow she'd worked for Billy's chair. At the coffee table he'd built with Truitt lumber. At the wood stove that kept her warm. At the photo of her and Billy on the wall by the door. Finally the gleam left her eyes and she shook her head. "No'm," she said, almost in a shout, calling Mom back from the bedroom. "I thanks you, but I won't come. This is my place, and Billy's. I'll stay." She was speaking quietly now. "You understand, ma'am."

There must have been something there in the cabin she and Billy had built. Something in the air, in the fresh smell from the garden, in the creak of the floorboards, in the shadowy memories, that meant more to her than life.

Mom stood still. "All right, Laurabell," she said quietly.

It didn't make sense, Laurabell's staying there. She could have brought her things with her. She was being plain stubborn. Still, there was a firmness about the lift of her chin, the set of her mouth, that made me admire her for sticking up for herself, even though it was kind of crazy.

ELEVEN

At Piney Pond the next day, they could talk about me all they liked. They could sympathize with Cade about the way I'd corrupted Dennis, and halfway pushed her into falling so she'd lost her precious dignity, and been seen with Abby Winch. They could spend all afternoon and evening at it if they liked. I felt bad about missing my lesson with Dennis. Otherwise I didn't care. Not much, anyway.

Maybe they'd miss me. Maybe they'd wish I was there.

That night I had a dream. Cade was a fish, maybe a mermaid. She was splashing around what might have been Piney Pond, smiling at me, waving her arms once in a while, making sparkles on the water. Now and then she'd disappear, and after a minute she'd surface in another spot and thrash around some more. I felt like going out to her, but I couldn't budge. My boots were as heavy as concrete, and somehow I felt that Abby was behind me, watching. All of a sudden Cade's smile changed to a frown. She dove into the water and disappeared. I woke up shivering and stared at the murky green stripes in my wallpaper, feeling sweaty and miserable.

It took a long time for the feeling to go away. I slept in fits and starts. Finally the low voices of the truck drivers out in the yard woke me again. I listened to the rocket sounds of their engines whirring into action and watched the dawn easing into my room, and I felt safe again. I was back in my world.

I got up and padded across the room and took the latest snapshots out of my top desk drawer. The one I'd taken of Cade bringing in the wind-surfer had come out sharp and clear. Her arms and legs were smooth and shiny with drops of water, and her eyes were crinkled and half smiling at me. She was happy and alive, and I ached that I'd lost the part of her that had given me so much fun. She and I might have gone to live in Boston someday. Or maybe even New York. Someplace exciting.

Later that morning I called Rusty to tell him not to pick me up for Piney Pond. "What gives?" he asked.

"I'm not going where I'm not wanted. Tell Dennis I'm sorry about the lesson. I'm really sorry."

"Okay, Truitt. See ya." He hadn't even tried to persuade me to change my mind. Well, what are friends for?

It was hot when I tossed my backpack into the rear seat of the Nova and picked up Abby for the drive to Scrubtop Mountain. On her way out, she broke off a daisy from the roadside, and in the car she held it up to my face. "It says good morning to you, Paige."

Sheez! I shifted into gear and stepped on the gas.

I slowed down as I drove through Huntville and on

toward Scrubtop. The road curved around from the steep east side, where a trailer stood in a clearing with a blue '79 Valiant out in front. We parked in the mountain's shadow, on the west side, near where Mrs. Ober lives. I waved to her as she pounded a tomato stake into the ground. She stopped to wipe a wisp of gray hair out of her sharp blue eyes and gave us an inspection. "Morning, Paige. You taking a climb?"

"Right, Mrs. Ober." I hurried Abby toward the trail. I didn't feel like answering questions. Mrs. Ober's okay, but she's an awful gossip. Her Labrador barked at us but didn't bother to get up. He was getting old, like his mistress.

For any blueberries that might have come out, I'd brought an old beach pail, which I'd given to Abby to carry while I shifted the lunch into my backpack. The trail smelled of pine and rotting wood and mold. About halfway up the mountain, it petered out. There were only rocks, scrub pines, bellflowers, grasses, blueberry bushes, and patches of crumbly soil. Abby found more and more berries as we climbed. It was hard to keep myself from laughing out loud at her excitement. "Here, Paige, have some," she'd say, holding out a small handful, with her voice leaving an echo in the air. The berries were almost like buckshot, small and dark and hard. But I'd take two or three to humor her. Probably we'd both get stomachaches.

Scrubtop isn't exactly Mount Everest. All you need to make the top from the west side is a decent pair of gym shoes to get you over the smooth rocks. Abby ate about every fifth berry she found. She kept pushing her bangs aside to get them out of her eyes, but they'd only fall back down. "Listen to the birds," she said. "They must be getting sore throats."

We had been climbing about an hour when she popped another berry into her mouth, swallowed, and said, "Is it on account of me that Cade's mad at you?"

"Who said she was still mad at me?"

"It's perfectly obvious. It explains why she was so horrid to me. It wasn't necessary for you to retaliate the way you did, however. I saw what you did."

"Mm, well, I'm not too proud of myself. I was boiling mad, though. And Cade's a pill. I never knew she could get so jealous, but we learn these things one at a time. Shucks, if the world doesn't spin around her, she gets furious. I guess she's been saying things about me that are pretty mean. Sheez! I haven't done anything to her."

Abby didn't bring up the fact that I had defended Cade to her before. She said, "I feel bad about what she's doing, Paige. You know I didn't intend for it to happen."

"I know."

She leaned over to check out a blueberry bush. "Everything's going to be all right, though. You're not the kind of person who gets pushed around. I'll bet the whole mess will blow over before school starts. People will come to their senses and realize how reprehensible she is."

"Sure," I said sarcastically. "I can hardly wait."

I wished I had as much faith in human nature as she did.

We reached the mountaintop, tired and hot and puffing, at around eleven-thirty. The sun was almost directly over us. I set the backpack on a smooth rock, and Abby put the pail beside it, about a third full of berries. We sat and looked out at the higher mountains in the distance, breathing in the fresh air, listening to the stillness. "It's nice," said Abby. "Those mountains. That view. Just being here. It's something you can hang on to. It's permanent."

"Nothing's permanent."

"It can be, for you, if you make it that way." She hugged herself, swaying back and forth with her excitement. "Thanks for bringing me, Paige. It's magnificent. I've fallen in love with every rock and bush and tree. I'm completely transported."

"Have you got to talk like that?"

"Like what?"

"Using those big, dumb words like *magnificent* and *transported*."

She dropped her shoulders. She seemed to shrivel and turn into a small child. I'd done it again. "It is too magnificent," she blurted out. "Can't you see? Can't you even see?"

I looked again. Everything in sight was washed in sunshine. The nearer mountains sparkled deep green, with the outlines of the New Hampshire peaks bald and clear. Below us, on Scrubtop, were groves of pines, with sparrows and goldfinches chasing each other, breaking the hush with their chirping. A shiver went through me.

I turned to see Abby, her chin forward on her knees, her eyes pushed shut, a ball of misery. Suddenly I wanted to reach out and comfort her. But I had to watch myself. She was no high school kid. She was young and vulnerable. It was up to me to keep my head on straight so we'd both stay out of trouble. "Hey, I'm sorry," I said. "It's that business about acting intelligent, isn't it?" In spite of myself, I patted her shoulder. Her hair was soft, like a cloud.

"*Help!*"

There was a voice behind us, so faint we barely seemed to have heard it, and yet I felt a chill.

"Help! Please help!"

I sat up straight and turned in the direction of the sound. There was silence, and the voice came again. "I'm stuck. Please help me." The voice broke.

It was a young voice, coming from the steep east slope where no one with any sense ever climbed. Whoever it was must have heard us talking. "All right," I shouted. "I'm coming."

Abby followed me to the crest of Scrubtop, and from there we looked down and saw him.

TWELVE

It was a chubby boy around nine wearing a dirty red T-shirt and jeans. He stood on a narrow ledge of rock just above the tree line with his body pressed against the mountainside, maybe the length of a football field away. His left hand was wound around a clump of grass, and he had thrown his head back so he was looking up at us, squinting into the sun. His face was streaked. From dirt and tears, I supposed. Two or three feet above his head was a scrub pine with a trunk a couple of inches across.

The boy looked husky enough. He must have climbed from below onto the ledge, been unable to reach the tree, and been afraid to let himself down. The ledge was about a foot wide, with only room for him to stand. He must be exhausted.

Should we go for help? Probably there wasn't time. The boy might topple at any minute. I shouted at him. "Don't worry. We'll get you out of there." I tried to sound upbeat, knowing he needed hope.

The boy said nothing. He only kept his eyes on me as if I might disappear. I looked down at the face of the mountain. There weren't many footholds. I wasn't sure I could make it, but I had to try. "It won't take long," I called, trying to keep my voice calm. Still, it sounded hollow in the emptiness. "Just be patient, okay? Keep leaning forward. You're doing fine."

The boy nodded.

Abby started to come with me. "You'd better stay here," I said.

"I will not. I'm coming."

"Listen, Abby, if there's any trouble, someone would have to run for help. You have to stay."

"But you can't do that by yourself."

"I've got to."

"Mm, well..." She ran her tongue around her lips. "Well, all right, I guess. But Paige, you have to be extremely careful. Will you, Paige? Please, Paige?"

"Don't worry," I said. "Just don't worry." I didn't want to make her any more frightened than she was.

Slowly I scrambled my way toward the boy, kicking dirt out from between the rocks to get a toe in. I zigzagged, looking for footholds, holding on to saplings. "Don't look down," I told myself. "And keep going. Just keep going." Still, I thought more than once of giving up.

Now and then I called out to the boy. "Take it easy. Easy, boy. It's okay. Just hold steady." Whenever I managed to look at him, his eyes were staring at me.

"We've got a picnic up here," called Abby. "Baked chicken. You can have some when you get here."

Twice I nearly fell. And once I stumbled and hit my left knee against a rock. Finally, as I got near him, I heard the boy's breath coming in gasps. Made out the tear streaks on his grubby face. Saw his reddish nose, and the blood marks on his hands from his scrambling in the dirt. There were ridges in the patches of crumbling earth above him where he must have tried to get a handhold. He was shaking from the effort of holding himself up.

Below him was a drop of several feet. There was a sapling directly under his rock that had partly come out by the roots. He must have stood on it to climb to the ledge and pulled it out with his weight.

By the time I got near his left side, my knee was throbbing. I knew the hard part was ahead of us. I forced myself to smile. "You got a name?"

He swallowed. His teeth were all but chattering. "Malcolm P-Percival," he said softly. He had tight blond curls like the kernels on a corn cob. A chipped front tooth. Blue eyes. Patches of a face slightly burned by the sun showing through the dirt. He must be a city boy. How had he come to be here?

"I'm Paige, and that's Abby up there. Now, Malcolm, can you follow directions? Because you've got to do exactly what I say."

He nodded again, gritting his teeth.

I reached for the scrub pine above him. "Now, edge over to your right so I can stand next to you." I hoped the tree was strong enough to hold me. And, thank goodness, it bent only a little way as I let myself down next to Malcolm. "I'll lift you up, Malcolm, and you latch onto that tree. Think you can do that?"

He looked up. His eyes went round. Finally he said, "Okay."

"Good boy. Now, don't wiggle."

It was awkward for me to lift him, keeping my weight on my right foot. I took hold of his left arm, worked my right hand between his legs, and edged him up an inch at a time. He was heavy. "Reach up, Malcolm. Keep reaching."

His fingers touched the tree. I wasn't sure I could lift him an eighth of an inch higher. My arms ached. My left knee throbbed. My feet were numb. I shifted my hand to his rear end, and somehow I gradually managed so his fingers were high enough to grab the trunk. He'd made it. "Good. That's good, Malcolm." I was breathing hard, almost gasping. "Now see if you can put your foot between those rocks right there."

He did. And I guided him over my zigzag route toward the top, getting him to step in the holes I had made on the way down, encouraging him. "That's great, Malcolm, just great."

Once I made the mistake of looking down. The emptiness seemed to go on forever. It seemed to be whirling, making me dizzy. Quickly, I forced myself to focus on Malcolm. "You're doing fine, Malcolm."

When we were getting toward the top, his foot slipped. He began to fall backward. Automatically, I reached over and shoved him against the rock. My grip loosened on the bush I was holding in my left hand. I wobbled backward. Lost my balance.

"*Paige!*"

Abby's scream pulled me back. Somehow I managed to tighten my fingers. Somehow I held us steady.

Malcolm and I were still, with our breath coming in gasps against the side of the mountain.

"Ooh, gol!" he muttered. "Ooh, gol!"

Finally I could talk. "You okay, Malcolm?"

"I can't go on. I just can't." He was sniffling.

"Sure you can. You have to."

"You can do it," called Abby. "You're almost here."

"Come on, Malcolm," I said. "You ready?"

Finally, after a minute, he nodded. I got him going again, inching along slowly, never taking my eyes off him except to make sure my own feet wouldn't slide. Those last few yards seemed to take years.

Abby's face was white. "You're a real mountain climber, Malcolm," she called out. She reached toward him. "Take my hand." She guided him onto the firm ground at the top, where he plopped onto a patch of grass and dirt.

He began to shake harder than ever. His teeth chattered. Abby hugged him. "You're all right now, Malcolm. You're perfectly all right. You're just worn out. Everything's fine, though, Malcolm." She went on and on in a singsong voice, almost crooning, until finally Malcolm relaxed.

But I wondered if he'd ever be the same again.

THIRTEEN

I was pooped. There was a stabbing pain in my knee, and my hands ached. I flopped on the ground beside Abby. But even with all the tiredness and pain, I felt great. I hadn't blown it. I'd done it. Me, Paige Truitt. I think I must have smiled, almost laughed, from being proud and relieved.

"Malcolm," said Abby, "how did you get up there?" She'd brought the backpack and was wiping some of the dirt off his hands and face with a napkin.

"I just climbed, that's all. And now I'm lost. I wanted to show my dad. See, I'm visiting my dad and his girl-friend in their trailer, and I wanted to show him I could climb a mountain. I wanted to show him..." His voice trailed off.

I sat up. "Well, we'll shovel some food into you and get you back to them. Bet they're worried about you." They must live in the new trailer at the foot of the mountain, the one Abby and I had seen on the way in. Mrs. Ober would know for sure.

"How did you get so high?" asked Abby. "That took a lot of climbing."

"Well, see, I just had to get to the top. And I did, didn't I?" He actually gave a faint smile.

"You two must be exhausted," said Abby.

"Right," said Malcolm. "I was sure I was going to fall, and no one would ever know what happened to me till they found my bones."

Once he'd started talking, he only stopped to eat. He talked, between bites of chicken, all during our picnic. "I'm from Worcester," he said. "Worcester, Massachusetts. I never get lost in Worcester, but I'm lost here, aren't I? My mom works in a hospital in Worcester, and I can hardly wait to get back. I hate it here."

I felt myself stiffen. Funny. It was all right for me to be tired of the place where I lived, but now that an outsider was trashing it, I was upset. "It's not so bad," I said.

"Oh, the place is okay. It's only that I'm lonesome without my friends and my—" He bit his lip.

Abby offered him a carrot stick. "I'll bet you miss your mom. My mom is a million miles away, and I miss her too."

He took a deep breath, stared straight ahead, and snapped off a bite of carrot stick.

Abby pointed to the mountains across the border and giggled. "Don't the tops of those mountains look as if they'd been shaved?" She was right. From this distance, the heads were smooth and dark. She handed us each a Mac. "I love fresh apples," she said. "They're so flavorful."

Since there wasn't one for her, I got out my Swiss army knife, cut mine in two, and tucked half of it into her hand behind Malcolm's back. He was busy talking.

After my morning, the apple didn't taste bad. I'd been eating them practically since the day I was born, but I'd never realized how, um, flavorful they can be.

The pain in my knee was less awful now, and I managed to get down Scrubtop without having Abby notice I was favoring my left leg. If she hadn't been preoccupied with Malcolm, she surely would have. We reached Mrs. Ober's house around two-thirty. She was sitting in the rocker on her front porch fanning her face with a flier from the hardware store. Her dog, who lay beside her, lifted his head. We walked past the vegetable garden, past the crooked row of tomato vines. "Afternoon, Mrs. Ober," I said, grinning. "Would you happen to know where this boy's dad lives?"

The rocker creaked as she leaned forward to take a look at Malcolm's streaked face. "He lost?"

"Yup."

"Paige rescued me," said Malcolm. "I was pretty near the top on the other side, and I got stuck and couldn't move. I was there for hours."

"Poor child." She set the flier on the arm of the rocker. "He rescued you on the east side? Well, I'll be! That slope's desperate steep, especially near the top."

"It's awful," said Abby. She insisted on giving every last detail of the rescue, while I looked at the ground and felt my face flush.

Mrs. Ober kept shaking her head. "Well, now, Paige, I declare you're a regular hero. What you did was near impossible."

"Nah. Anybody could've done it, Mrs. Ober."

"They could not," said Abby. "You were spectacular."

Without my tan I was sure my face would have been apple red. "Look, we've got to get Malcolm home. Those folks will be frantic."

Mrs. Ober inspected Malcolm. "I expect you're visiting those new people in the trailer 'round the mountain, aren't you, young fellow? Name begins with a *P.*"

"Right. It's a trailer, and it's somewhere over there, and I'm Malcolm Percival. I'm visiting my dad."

I took his arm. "So long, Mrs. Ober. Thanks for the information."

We hurried to the car.

Out in the front of the trailer, a man was kneeling to check a tire on the Valiant. He was about thirty-five. Five-eleven. Blond beard and mustache. Big clown hands and feet. Red face. T-shirt with GIORGIO'S PIZZA across the front. The sound of a crying baby came from inside. Then silence, and a blurry face at the trailer window. The man squinted at us as Malcolm bounded out of the Nova. "Hi, Dad."

"Hi, there, Malcolm, you roll in the dirt? Where you been, anyhow?"

"Haven't you missed me? I was up on the mountain. Up on top. These people—Well, we found each other up there." Apparently Malcolm had decided not to tell his father the details.

The father stood up and came forward, narrowing his eyes at us. "Hasn't your mom taught you not to take rides with strangers?"

"But Dad, these people are okay. They—"

"Don't do that again, son."

Malcolm turned to us, biting his lip. He swallowed.

"Thanks a lot," he said in a soft, husky voice. "Thanks."

"Take care of yourself, Malcolm." I stepped on the accelerator and took off.

Abby fumed. "Can you believe it, Paige? They didn't even miss him. They didn't even worry."

"Look, we can't be sure. Maybe they thought he'd gone out for a long walk along the road. They probably figured he'd be home soon."

"But he missed his dinner. They might have known a boy like him would get hungry. That man is his father, Paige, but he's so tied up with his girlfriend and their baby he can't be bothered with Malcolm. The whole situation exasperates me. I wish we could do something."

"We did do something. We did all we could. He'll be going back to his mom soon anyway."

"But circumstances like that make you feel so helpless."

"I know." I squeezed her hand. After the experience we had shared, I felt closer to her. "You were great, Abby. Wouldn't have made it without you."

I drove along, feeling the warmth. After a few minutes, she said, "You really do love this place, Paige."

"What makes you think so?"

"I saw how bothered you were when Malcolm said he hated it. I don't think you half know how precious it is to you, and that's because you've always lived here. It's familiar to you, so you don't think about it. But it's in your bones, Paige."

Maybe. And maybe not. I didn't want to think about it. What sense was there in loving this crummy blacktop road we were on, or the rocks and grasses and weeds in the fields, or the pesky chipmunks and porcupines, or the work on the farm that never ends?

"What's it like here in the spring?" she asked.

What could I tell her? "Well, it's sort of nice after the winter. Winters are long, you know, and you can hear coyotes, sometimes awfully close. But when the apple blossoms come out, they're good to look at."

"They must be magnificent. I'll bet the hills look like fairyland."

"Mm, yeah. They're some pretty."

"Are the winters really all that horrible?"

"Well, there's snow. Piles of it. But we get out the snowmobiles and race around. And sometimes a bunch of us will go skiing over to Bethel. They've got great slopes there. Afterward we come home and get warm next to a wood fire and watch the snow come down outside. It's fun warming up after you've been out in the cold."

"Paige, you love this place. You do."

I hadn't intended to sound so enthusiastic. As I slowed the car to pass through Huntville, I turned and gave her an embarrassed smile. "Look, I never said I hated it." I thought about the Hill. The freshness of the air, and the way the wind ripples the leaves and grasses, and the look of the mountains on guard.

Abby laughed. "I'll bet if I asked you another time, you'd admit it's like a part of you."

"So ask me tomorrow."

Was she right about me? I had to wonder.

She looked back at the mountains. "Paige, I'll never forget today. I'll especially never forget your gallant deed, even though Mr. Percival didn't appreciate it."

At least Mrs. Ober had appreciated it. She'd called me a hero. A tune hummed inside me. But suddenly the tune stopped on a sour note. Telling something to Mrs. Ober was like telling it to the town crier. The news would be all over in no time. Everyone would fuss over me, especially the women. I'd rather tangle with a porcupine than get fussed over.

And Dad. Would he think I was a hero? And why did I care, anyhow?

FOURTEEN

The Winches broke the news to my family after church the next morning. "Looks as if we've got a hero on this hill," said Grampa at dinner.

Mom's eyes shone. "Why didn't you tell us, Paige? That was some rescue! I suppose that's how you banged that knee of yours."

So she had noticed.

"It's nothing, Mom. I can barely feel it now." This wasn't exactly true, but the knee did feel better.

Joyce beamed. "You were terrific, Paige. That east side of Scrubtop is near straight up and down."

"Nice going, Paige," said Dad in a husky voice. "Makes me think of the time my granddad fished a man out of the river in near darkness."

I must have heard that story a hundred times. The man had tipped his boat over in the river, near the bridge in the village, and Great-Grampa scrambled down the bank and rescued them both, the man and the boat. I was glad Dad was pleased with me, but why did he have to bring in my ancestors?

"I've heard the story, Dad."

"Well, you ought to be proud of it. You're part of a tradition, Paige."

"Big deal. Look, I'm taking a pass. I didn't rescue that kid on account of any tradition."

"Paige!" It was Mom, with her mouth tight and her eyes narrowed in hurt.

"I didn't ask to be a Truitt, Mom. I do things on my own, not because somebody in my family did something wonderful way back when the world was flat."

There was silence. Joyce opened her mouth to speak, and closed it. Grampa stared at his plate. Mom shut her eyes. Dad's jaw tightened. I'd gone too far.

Finally Dad cleared his throat. "I only meant to praise you, Paige."

"I know. It's just that sometimes I wish I'd been born an orphan."

Joyce giggled. "Nobody gets born an orphan, silly. And the world was never flat."

"Think I don't know that, mushbrain?"

She stuck her tongue out at me and then smiled. Dad's face broke into a grin. I couldn't keep from grinning back. The air was cleared. At least I hoped so. I hoped Dad understood how I felt. With him I never know.

By Monday the pain in my knee was nearly gone. The news of the rescue had reached all over the village. We were digging a trench for some new irrigation pipes, and the men at work kidded me about my amazing feat. "Now we know how come you weren't at Piney Pond on Saturday," said Harvey with his frog grin. "You were busy making yourself into a celebrity."

The others laughed, but they looked at me respect-fully. "Heard the kid was pretty husky." "Couldn't have been easy to handle him." "Ledge was some narrow, huh? Six inches, maybe?"

"Keep talking, you guys." I shook my head, laugh-ing. "Nah. The ledge wasn't all that narrow." I leaned on my shovel. The fuss was making me uncomfortable, and yet I couldn't help feeling proud. It was a tempta-tion to throw my shoulders back and brag a bit. They say it's not really bragging if you actually did the thing. But I resisted. "Look, it was nothing any of you strong, tough guys wouldn't have done."

And thank goodness for Abby.

Later on, Harvey paused in his digging and wiped sweat from his forehead. "What's happening, Truitt? How come you weren't at the pond Saturday?"

I shrugged. "Didn't feel like going. Didn't think I'd be welcome."

"We missed you."

"Bet Cade didn't miss me."

He gave me a quick look. "What's going on between her and you? She's been making up to me like I was caramel cake."

"Beats me." I looked away and took hold of my shovel. I might as well say it. "Anyway, you can have her." Something pulled at my insides when I heard those words come out. It made me sad, giving up on Cade after so many years. I dug my shovel into the dirt. "You know how she likes to run the show, and I guess she's discovered she can't run me."

"Well, she's not going to run me, I tell you."

Maybe not. And maybe so.

"I know I'm second choice," he said.

I dumped the dirt next to the trench. I said, "You're first choice now."

"Nah. If there wasn't something wrong between you two, she'd never have made a play for me. Not that I mind."

Through the sadness, I felt sorry for him, taking to Cade like that. He was headed for problems.

"What's really going on between you two?" he asked.

"Nothing much. Don't imagine she thinks much of Abby, though."

"So that's it. Well, I'll tell you, it wasn't near as much fun with you gone."

The news made the *Milton Times*. One of their reporters had heard it from someone who knew Mrs. Ober and called my mother for verification. She gave him the Winches' number, and Abby passed on a description of my heroic actions in the face of horrible danger. When the Monday paper came, it was on page two under the headline DARING MOUNTAIN RESCUE. I squirmed as I read the article. "Paige Truitt, 15, a resident of Bartlett, and a companion, Abby Winch, 13, were picnicking on Scrubtop Mountain when they heard the screams of Malcolm Percival, 9...." The story went on to tell how I stood on a six-inch ledge over a fifteen-foot drop, lifted Malcolm three feet to a tree, and eventually "returned the frightened boy to his distraught father, Hugh Percival, a resident of Huntville for the past six months." Abby had, of course, exaggerated the story. For one thing I hadn't lifted

Malcolm more than a foot, although it had seemed like ten.

Cade called that evening. "Paige, you're a celebrity. We're all so excited."

"There's nothing to be excited about, Cade. The article got it all wrong."

"Quit being so modest. I always knew you were a brave person, and now you've proved it."

"Look, I'm sorry I bumped you. It was a mean trick."

"Well, I probably deserved it. But how come you didn't come to the pond Saturday?"

"I won't be coming anymore. I don't feel like it."

"You don't *feel* like it?" An edge had oozed into her voice. "But Paige, you've got to. We were all talking about you, wondering where you were. We were worried about you."

If they'd had as little interest as Rusty, they hadn't been worrying very hard. But now that I'd been made into a hero, Cade wanted me back. I waited ten beats, took a breath, and said, "If I came, I'd bring Abby with me. If she'd come."

"Paige, she's such a baby."

"She is not. She's very mature." Sheez! What would I come out with next?

There was a pause. "Well," said Cade uncertainly, "I just don't think she'd enjoy being with us. We wouldn't have anything in common."

"So let's forget it," I said quickly. "Thanks for calling, Cade. No hard feelings, huh?"

"Of course not." She didn't sound awfully sure.

"See you around." I cut the connection.

I'd miss being with Cade. I still felt a pull when I thought of her.

It's funny how hard it is to recognize the snotty side of somebody till that person gets around to snubbing you personally. Harvey was all right, and Rusty too. They all were. Rusty hadn't meant to be thoughtless. Back at school this fall, I'd want to be friends with each of them, even Cade. I was sorry for her, knocking other people to build herself up, but I supposed she was only being human.

On the first day of August, a Saturday, Abby and I walked over to Laurabell's with a basket of food, including a thermos of Mom's vegetable soup and a bowl of Mrs. Winch's caramel custard. When we got near to Laurabell's cabin, the sound of Callie's meowing came to us through the trees. As we stepped into the clearing, we saw her standing at the edge of the garden with her head raised, as if she were begging us to hurry. And then we saw why.

Laurabell was seated in her sunset chair wearing a cotton robe over her nightie. Her head was slumped forward, and her arms hung loose over the arms of the chair. I set the basket down and ran to her, with Abby and Callie behind me. I knelt and lifted Laurabell's head. It was cold, with still eyes staring out of her skull face.

"She's dead, isn't she?" whispered Abby at last.

She couldn't be. But she was. I felt helpless and numb, breathing in the sour smell of death. I'd known the same feeling before. When I was five, there was Gramma. And over the years there were special pets.

But that was then, and this was now, and this was Laurabell.

For a long minute I stayed still, fighting the truth. Then I heard Abby's soft sobs. I stood and put my arms around her and held her close.

Abby stayed with Laurabell and Callie while I sprinted along Laurabell's dirt road and started up the farm road toward a phone. Luckily Sam Winch, driving up the hill on his way home from the village, caught up with me. I told him the news. "I'll go in and take a look," he said. "You and Abby drive my car home and call the rescue unit for the ambulance."

"But she's dead, Sam."

"Makes no difference. We'll need the ambulance anyhow. I'll go to the cabin and send Abby out to you. That's no place for a young girl."

Sam's a member of the village volunteer rescue unit and knows what to do. It was a relief to have him take over and to know the pressure was off me. I still felt awful, though. I still get the shivers when I think of that time.

As the hours and days passed, more and more people heard the news, until, at the memorial service on Friday evening, the village church was half filled with people who remembered Laurabell, some of whom remembered Billy. While we mingled outside afterward, most of the others came to shake the hands of Mom and Dad. Rusty's mother dabbed at tears. "I know it's a blessing. I'd heard she was poorly. But that won't make you miss her any the less."

Mrs. Biggs came next. She shook her head so the

feather on her hat waved like a droopy flag and took
Mom's hand in both of hers. "Lou, that woman loved
you and Ned, and that's a fact."

Abby, standing at my side, said, "You must feel
awful. You look sad." Still, she looked as sad as I must
have.

I did feel awful. I felt empty. I'd miss joking with
Laurabell. Laughing at her funniness. Being surprised
at how strong she was inside.

As we walked away, Abby said, "Is there anyone in
this place who's got any faults?"

I almost broke into a smile. "For pete's sake, Abby,
are you serious?"

"Of course I'm serious. Everyone is so *good*. I mean,
look at your mom and dad and your grampa and my
grandparents and Joyce and the way she smiles. Look
at Mrs. Garrison and Mrs. Biggs and Rusty's mom.
They're always exchanging food and recipes and rally-
ing around when someone gets sick or dies. They're all
so comfortable and wholesome and doing for each
other."

She was right. They are. They're also gossipy and
vain, and sometimes mean and petty. Some are just
plain rotten. But most people around here mean well.
They do try. "Maybe it's because we know each other.
Because we're stuck with each other."

"And you depend on each other."

Abby has a way of putting her finger on things.

Naturally, Laurabell's affairs had to be taken care of.
Abby had brought Callie to the Winch house and
adopted her. And since Joyce had long-standing plans

to go to the shore with her friends the day after the service, Mom conned me into driving with her to Laurabell's to go through her belongings. "The Salvation Army's the place for them," said Mom, "though goodness knows we'll probably be throwing most of them away. I don't suppose Laurabell bought anything new for years."

Laurabell's marigolds, in their stone-edged beds, were drooping from lack of water. We walked into the cabin with folded cartons from the packing house. The floorboards creaked, the refrigerator hummed, and yet the place seemed deathly quiet. "Now, Paige," said Mom, all business, "you take the bedroom while I do this main room. Use one carton for throw-away and one for give-away."

In the clothes closet there were a blanket, three summer dresses, two pairs of wool slacks, three heavy work shirts, Laurabell's wool coat and knitted cap, two pairs of shoes, and her old fleece-lined boots. In the bureau I found yellowed letters tied together, with Mississippi return addresses. I found pants and slips with holes and rips in the seams, stockings with runs, her navy-blue sweater coming unraveled along the bottom. I saved the letters to give to Mom. If Laurabell had any relatives left, Mom would want to write them. The clothes I distributed in the boxes.

I took the pills from the windowsill by the bed and dumped them into the toilet. The bed was unmade. The sheets and pillowcase were a mass of patches and mends. I picked up the pillow. Underneath was a book. Black, with gold letters on the front and on the spine. It was the Bible from Bible Corner.

To make sure I wasn't dreaming, I leafed through it. Sure enough. There was the piece of the page from the original Bible.

So it was Laurabell. *Laurabell.*

FIFTEEN

"She stole this Bible, Abby. There's no other explanation. She must have."

"Now, you listen to me, Paige Truitt, you're being ridiculous, and you've got to calm down. Laurabell wouldn't steal. It wasn't in her to steal."

"Believe me, I don't want to think she did. But you know it didn't grow legs and walk over to her place."

Mom had dropped me off at the Winches' to leave carrots and corn from Laurabell's garden while she went home to get supper. Abby had come to the door. "Let's go ask Grampa," she suggested. "I'll bet he can knock some sense into you."

It wasn't fair of her to say that. I *was* being sensible. Sheez! Did she imagine I enjoyed thinking Laurabell was a thief?

There were dabs of orange in a couple of the maples at the side of the road. Another ten days and August would be over. Next month the pickers would be here. And Abby would be gone. The thought gave me an empty feeling.

Grampa was in the kitchen making himself a sandwich for supper. "Paige," he said, "your face would sour milk."

When we'd explained about the Bible to him, he shook his head. "Hard to believe she stole that book. It's near impossible. But I've got no good answer for you, so I'll just put it back where it was and let the whole thing be. It's only a store-bought Bible anyhow."

I wasn't satisfied. We had a mystery on our hands, and there had to be a solution. Otherwise I'd always wonder. I had to put to rest my doubts about Laurabell. "Did Laurabell know about Bible Corner, Grampa?"

He pulled his eyebrows together as he buttered some bread. "Well, now that you mention it, I'm not right sure she did. I don't recall I ever mentioned it to her. Someone else might have, of course. Did you, Paige?"

"No. I figured she knew."

"I'll bet nobody told her," said Abby, sounding positive. "I'll bet you all thought she'd heard it from someone else, when she hadn't. And I'll bet she just happened to find that Bible one day while she was out walking."

"But you don't just find something that's kept inside a bunch of stones," I said. "Hey, remember, Abby? Remember that some of the stones had been taken away? She must have done that, because there was only a hole there, and the stones had disappeared. I wish there were another explanation, but there's not."

Abby nodded slowly. "She probably carried them in her skirt. But why would she take the stones too?"

We might never find the answer to that puzzle. But I needed to. I had to remember Laurabell well.

* * *

Back home, Dad was pulling into the barn from a trip to the Perrys' with the check for their apples. Mom called from the doorway. "How's Amos, Ned? Any better?"

Dad chuckled. "He is now. He was some happy to see that check. Might help with those doctor bills of his. I tell you it near killed me to part with that money, but it brought me back to life when I saw his face." He turned to me. "You've got to be square, Paige. No matter how much it hurts, always be square in your dealings. That way you can look your neighbor in the eye."

I already knew that. I knew that if you live in a village the way we do, there's always talk. But if you're in a city, you don't have to worry so much about ethics. So if I were to stay on the farm, I'd have to be careful. Did I want that?

Dad stood smiling at me, sure of himself, satisfied with his life. I didn't know if I could ever be like him. I felt wobbly, knowing what he expected of me.

Still, if I should decide to run this place, which I probably wouldn't, I'd have my family behind me. I'd know that what they were doing had worked, year after year. That each generation had taken the good part of what had been left to it and built on it, mixing the old and the new. I wouldn't be alone.

I smiled back at Dad. He rested his hand on my shoulder. Then, quickly, he cleared his throat, turned, and hurried to the door, where Mom was waiting for him.

On Saturday evening, Earl gave Joyce her ring. She showed it to us at breakfast the next morning, giving us that melting smile of hers. "Isn't it gorgeous? Isn't it the most beautiful thing you ever saw?" Her face was flushed.

The diamond looked like the head of a pin, but if she was happy I guess that was all that mattered. I imagined she knew how long Earl had saved to buy the ring. Mom managed to smile. "It's lovely, Joyce." She reached out and squeezed Joyce's hand. There were tears in her eyes.

Joyce sighed. "I know, Mom. He'll never be rich or famous. I've tried to talk myself out of marrying him, but I can't do it."

Dad said nothing at first. He took off his glasses, folded the bows in, set them on the table, and stared. Joyce threw him a smile, and he gave a shadowy smile in return. "You've got plans, I suppose."

"Uh-huh. We're getting married in June, the Saturday after graduation. Earl will go on working for Mr. English, and I'll find a job somewhere."

"You'll pardon me for saying so, but your plans don't seem extra-sound. You got a place to live?"

"Oh, Dad, that's no trouble. We'll find a place. May I take my bed and bureau, Mom? We'd be careful of them."

"Of course you would."

Dad tapped his glasses on the table. "I hear Wade English is fixing to sell off his Exxon station."

"Yes, but—"

"Listen, Dad," I broke in, "Mr. English thinks a lot of Earl. Says he's a great mechanic, that he's got more business on account of him."

Dad raised his eyebrows. "That right? So how come

Wade's not turning the station over to him?"

"Earl turned it down," said Joyce. "He doesn't want to be a businessman. And he's sure to find a job somewhere else if he needs to. Paige is right, Dad. Earl's good, and he loves the work."

In a way I envied Earl. He knew exactly what he wanted to do with his life, and he wasn't haunted by a lot of ancestral funny business. His parents are divorced. His father lives in town and works for the power company, his mother is a saleswoman at Penney's at the Milton mall, and I'll bet he doesn't even know who his great-grandparents were.

It was fine for him not to be tied down, but was it right for me? I didn't know. Should I tell Dad I didn't know? Abby was right. It was true he ought not to push me to take over the farm, but it was also true that I owed it to him, and to myself, to let him know how I felt. This wasn't the time, though. Not right after Joyce had got engaged to Earl. I couldn't hand him and Mom their second disappointment in a row.

Harvey and Cade walked out of church that morning holding hands. So it was official. He'd replaced me in her life. He was the one she might marry after high school. Probably she'd go off and live somewhere else with him, raise a family. I wondered if she'd get to be five feet square like her mother. Now she was slim and graceful and shining. The old habit of caring was still stuck somewhere inside me, but it was dying.

Cade turned and looked, probably checking to make sure I'd seen them. I forced a smile and a wave, and they smiled and waved back.

After noon dinner, Grampa and Joyce helped Mom with the dishes, and Dad asked me to help set up cartons for the next day's packing. "They're behind on the orders, Paige."

Out in the packing house, I asked, "Am I getting paid?"

Dad put his hands on his hips and said in that gruff way of his, "Are Grampa and Joyce getting paid for helping your mother? For that matter, do your mother and I get paid?"

"You take your piece of the profits."

"And you benefit from that. You've got to learn, son, that when you run a business, you take the responsibility. You put in extra hours when they're needed, and you don't fuss about it."

There it was again, his assuming I'd be taking over. His attitude was getting on my nerves. I had to speak up. Now. Even though the timing was bad. If I didn't, the problem would only get worse.

I set my feet apart, swallowed, and looked him in the eye. "Dad, you can't count on me to run this place. I'm thinking of going to live in some city after college. Probably Boston."

He sucked his breath in and stared. He seemed to go limp, as if the air were slowly leaking out of him. He backed up to the conveyor belt and leaned against it. "Live? In Boston? You're putting me on, Paige." He was almost whispering.

Was he having a heart attack or something? Was he furious with me? Should I take back what I'd said? Only I had to tell him the truth. "I'm serious, Dad. I should have told you before, but you never asked me.

You took it for granted I'd take over. I've got the right to decide that."

He looked me up and down, as if I were a stranger. His eyes had gone misty. His lip trembled. "Boston," he said slowly. "How could anyone want to live there? You're bound to change your mind." He didn't want to imagine how it would be if I actually meant what I'd said.

He was having a tough day. First Joyce had disappointed him, and now I was doing the same. It must have seemed as if his world had fallen apart. But at least he hadn't blown up. I wished I could say something to make him feel better. "I'm sorry, Dad. But look, I only said I might go." Funny. I really wasn't sure. In fact, with Abby's help, I was learning to love this place. I was noticing things I'd ignored before. And it seemed that the fonder I grew of the farm, and the more I realized I had a choice, the readier I was to be honest with Dad.

He cleared his throat. "All right, Paige. I should have asked you. But I thought—" He broke off, removed his glasses, put them back on, rubbed his chin. He looked out through the door toward Grampa's house. "It's just that it's been going on for so long."

"I know. But don't you see? I've always felt trapped. I felt as if I didn't have any choice. But I do."

There was a long silence while he stared into space. Finally he gave a deep, shaking sigh. He came over and laid his hand on my shoulder and said in his gravelly voice, "You're right, Paige. You do."

SIXTEEN

Dad must have told Mom about our conversation. For the next few days she kept giving me glances, as if she were about to speak, but not speaking except for the usual everyday remarks. Then I came in from work one evening, all beat from thinning and mowing in Tinker Field, and flopped into the captain's chair by the desk with my boots out in front of me. Mom came out of the kitchen with plates, set them at Dad's place, walked over, and put her hand on my cheek. She hadn't done that for years. "I'm glad you spoke up, Paige," she said quietly. Her voice was husky.

I couldn't answer. I could feel her pain. But I knew she'd finally realized I was nearly grown. She and Dad had changed toward me. They'd been keeping their distance, treating me with more respect. More like a grownup. Their attitude scared me in a way, but in another way it propped up my ego, made me feel lighter.

After dinner the next Saturday noon, Dad scraped his chair back from the table, heaved himself to his feet, and said to Joyce, "With the poor apple crop, we can't afford new trucks, so we'll need more help in the mechanics' shop keeping the old ones going. You think Earl might like to work over there Saturdays after school starts?"

"Oh, Dad! You know that's what he wants, to be responsible for cars and trucks he can get to know. They'll be like friends to him. Look, I'll go call him right now. He'll be so excited."

"You tell him he'll be on trial. Say that if he does a decent job, it'll be full time come next summer."

"We thought you two might want Laurabell's cabin," said Mom. "Might as well put it to use, and you could be doing some painting and papering between now and June."

The color was rising in Joyce's face. "Mom, you're terrific. You're both terrific."

She jumped up and gave Mom a hug, and then Dad, who said in his rough voice, "We'll see if it works out. We'll see." He turned to me. "Checked out that irrigation system this morning, Paige. You men did a good job."

"Thanks, Dad." We grinned at each other, maybe seeing each other for the first time.

After a minute he clomped out, to go help Grampa caulk windows at the pickers' barracks. As he crossed the yard, with his boots crunching a fallen leaf here and there, his step was springy, and he held his head up, as if he'd made kind of a peace with himself.

"Mom," said Joyce, "was it your idea for us to have the cabin?"

Mom shrugged. It had been her idea, of course. She must have realized that if I decided not to take over the farm, there would be at least one member of our family still around. Two if you counted Earl.

Earl came over later that afternoon, and he and Joyce went to look at the cabin. I had a feeling Earl would make it here. He'd never want to run the place, but in the mechanics' shop he'd be respected and appreciated, and goodness knows he was needed. I didn't like to think of Mr. English's having to turn over his business to another person, maybe a stranger. Still, there was sure to be someone interested in it, maybe one of the people who'd moved up from town.

Earl came back to our place for supper, and as he gulped down a bite of tomato wedge, he said, "That cabin's okay. Good, sound materials. And the folks who built it sure knew how to build. Joyce says it was Laurabell and her husband."

"Billy," said Joyce. "I remember Billy. When I was little, he used to swing me around out in the yard." She sat twirling her fork. "That picture of him and Laurabell. If you've still got it, Mom, we'd like to hang it on the wall again if her relatives don't want it."

Mom had slipped it into our attic with some old family photographs, but she said, "No, the relatives didn't ask for it, so it's yours. I'll fetch it for you when the time comes."

"Thanks. We thought we'd paper the walls in a pale-blue-and-white stripe and lighten up the outside with a sort of cream color. . . ." She went on and on, while Earl sat nodding in that slow way of his. Nobody stopped them. In fact, Dad was all but smiling.

Joyce hunched her shoulders and hugged herself. "Ooh, it's so exciting. I'll keep the vegetable garden going and marigolds growing inside those rocks by the door, and we thought..."

The rocks. Hey, that was it. Laurabell must have been out with her basket looking for smooth rocks and found them at Bible Corner. The rocks there had begun to fall apart. They were loose, and she needed them. She'd decided they were of no use to anyone. And then she'd been surprised to find a Bible and decided it had somehow been left there and forgotten. Maybe she should have asked one of us about it, but she'd probably assumed we didn't know and didn't care. At any rate, she hadn't deliberately gone there knowing about it.

Thank goodness I had the explanation. I ought to pass it on to Abby.

Glad of an excuse to see her, I went down to the Winches' that evening past the row of old maples with the sun setting behind them and the clouds like pink streamers painted on the sky. Abby came to the door, with Callie mewing beside her. Abby had filled out over the summer. The angles of her face and body had softened. "Hello, Paige."

"I figured it out," I said. "Laurabell didn't take those rocks to get the Bible. She took them for her marigold beds. I don't think she knew that book was there. That's the key."

"Well, of course. She needed the rocks. We should have thought of that before."

"Well, thank goodness it finally came clear."

"Who is it, Abby?" called Mrs. Winch from inside.

"It's Paige, Grandmother."

"Well, don't leave him out there. Ask him in."

The Winches had plans to take Abby to a family re-
union in Alden later that evening. While Abby and I
helped them with the dishes, I found out that Sam
Winch had served in Italy in World War II and still had
shrapnel inside him. "It's in a pretty embarrassing
place," he said, chuckling. I also discovered that Mrs.
Winch had refinished and needlepointed a great set of
four chairs, each with a different bird design. And I
got the word that Abby would be leaving on Thursday
to go back to San Antonio.

August was nearly over. The summer had slipped
away from me little by little, like water dripping
through the cracks between my fingers. And Abby
would be gone. She was on the edge of growing up, but
I wouldn't see her do it. She was like a promise that, for
me, would never be kept.

As I left, she gave me her pixie grin. "Stop and tell
Grampa about the stones, Paige. He'll want to know."
All of a sudden she looked terrific, with her eyes mel-
low and her face soft and brown and warm. Now that
she was going, I pictured the hollow space she'd leave
in my life. No, that wasn't right. She'd leave a memory,
the way dreams do.

I nodded. At that moment I'd have done most anything for her.

Besides, I wanted to set things straight with Grampa.
Back I went through the stillness. When I passed
through Grampa's side door and into his living room,
taking care to make plenty of noise to warn him I was
there, I found him slumped in his easy chair with his
feet on the footstool Gramma had embroidered. The
Red Sox were on TV, but in spite of my racket Grampa

was sound asleep with his mouth open, breathing in snorts.

I sat on the sofa and watched Roger Clemens pitch a no-hit half inning before Grampa twisted in his chair, gave one loud snore, opened his eyes, and looked around, blinking. I grinned at him.

"Hello there, Paige. Say, what you doing hereabouts on a Saturday night?"

"I came to see you, Grampa." A beer commercial came on. "I wanted to tell you that Abby and I figured it out about the Bible." I explained about the rocks. "So Laurabell must have just happened to run across the Bible and decided nobody wanted it."

Grampa nodded. "Makes sense. Glad you figured it out, Paige. I wouldn't want you thinking she'd heard that story. At any rate there's no harm done. I set that Bible back in place, and it's a comfort to me knowing it's there."

It was a comfort to me too.

SEVENTEEN

Mrs. Winch was driving Abby to her plane early Thursday morning. The evening before, I strolled down the road. The leaves of the maples were rustling, and the sun was a ball in the west. At the Winch house, I asked Abby to go for a walk, and she came, wearing the too-big cardigan that had been her mother's. We tramped through the milkweed and goldenrod and Queen Anne's lace, across Puckett Field, and along the woods path that leads to the ledge where she and I had first met, and we sat on the log where I'd found her. We sat for a long time, surrounded by pine scent and the cooing of a mourning dove. Now and then we said a few words, as a way of touching.

The light in the church steeple was on, and more and more windows began to sparkle in the village. Stars popped out into the darkening sky. Finally Abby said, "I haven't even begun to pack. I couldn't somehow."

"So why leave? I'll bet your grandparents would love to keep you here."

She shook her head. "It's hard to explain. You see, my parents are awfully sophisticated. All glitzy and

trendy and pretending. They don't seem to really live."
I remembered thinking the same thing about my own
parents, the part about not really living. "I'll be all right
once I get home," she went on. "Dad and Mom do love
me in their careless way. I'm their pet. I'm like a sort of
magnet. If they didn't have me to come back to, they'd
go flinging themselves in all directions, breaking the
law of gravity, and they'd lose their way. They've had
their excitement, and now they need me to come home
to."

In some ways, Abby was a lot older than thirteen.
And yet she was young. I had to remember that.

I'd never known her father, who'd grown up here on
the Hill. Once in a while the Winches had made the
trip to San Antonio, but he hadn't ever come back. It
was hard to picture him as the son of the Winches. He
must be extra-bright and extra-ambitious, and hungry
to see the world. Was I hungry like that? I'm not wildly
ambitious, but I would like to see other places. Still, a
person can always travel.

Abby was saying, "Anyway, you won't miss me. You'll
be back in school with your friends."

I picked up a twig, snapped it, and pitched the pieces
over the ledge. "You ever going to come back?"

"I don't know. Maybe, someday. I'll be going away to
boarding school next year, so I suppose they'll want me
home in the summers as a sort of security blanket." She
looked up at me. "I want to come back, Paige."

"You won't, though. You'll forget all about me. Us."

"I'll never do that."

I wanted to thank her for her gift. For pricking me.
For making me see what was under my nose. "I'll miss

you, Abby." There was an ache in me, like a sad song. This was crazy. What was there about her? How could I be hypnotized by a brat of a girl with bangs all over her face?

I forced myself to stand up and reach out my hand to her. We walked along the path toward home, taking in the rustlings of the birds and animals and leaves that cut into the evening hush. We walked slowly, hoarding the minutes. I almost didn't dare look at her, at the way her hair was tousled by puffs of air, and the way her neck curved into her blouse, and the way she walked so lightly she seemed to be barely moving. Abby, with her pointed chin and her fuzzy voice and her eyes that go on and on.

The Winches' steps were worn down, like the sides of a row boat. They were newly painted. Gray. The brass knocker on the door was polished bright.

"So long, Paige."

"So long, Abby." I brushed aside her bangs, put my hands on her shoulders, and kissed her on the forehead. It wasn't right. It wasn't enough.

Her eyes were shiny with tears. Suddenly she threw her arms around me and pressed her head hard against my chest.

But only for a second. She pulled away, sniffling, and rushed inside, leaving me with my hands empty.

I held my breath, feeling the wet spot her tears had made on my shirt, staring at the door, maybe hoping it would open again.

It did. The tail of her sweater had caught in the door. She yanked it to her, almost angrily, and threw me a last, quick look, daring me to laugh, before she banged the door shut.

Silly, crazy Abby. There was no way I could laugh.

I scuffed down the steps and up the hill past Grampa's dark windows. In front of the Big House, I turned and stared out between the maples, over the tangled shadows of the apple trees, across the old section of the farm, to the outlines of the mountains.

I turned again to face the Big House, almost as if I'd never seen it before. It was familiar to me, and yet I knew so little about it. It had taken me a long time to understand even a part of why my father loves this place, and it had taken me years to discover I had a choice as to whether I'd stay. Now that I knew I had the choice, would I decide to stay? I might, I told myself. If you asked me tomorrow, I just might.

For Abby, of course.

And for me.